BAGTHORPES
ABROAD

BAGTHORPES ABROAD

Being the Fifth Part of The Bagthorpe Saga by

HELEN CRESSWELL

MACMILLAN PUBLISHING COMPANY
New York

Macmillan Publishing Company
866 Third Avenue, New York, N.Y. 10022
First American edition 1984
Printed in the United States of America
10 9 8 7 6 5 4 3 2 1

LIBRARY OF CONGRESS CATALOGING IN PUBLICATION DATA
Cresswell, Helen.
   Bagthorpes abroad.
   (Being the fifth part of the Bagthorpe saga)
   Summary: Chronicles the further adventures of the
eccentric Bagthorpe family as they go on vacation to a
reputedly haunted house in Wales.
   [1. Family life—Fiction. 2. Vacations—Fiction.
3. Wales—Fiction] I. Title. II. Series: Cresswell,
Helen. Bagthorpe saga (New York, N.Y.) ; 5th pt.
PZ7.C8645Baf 1984   [Fic]   84-7125
ISBN 0-02-725390-2

Also by Helen Cresswell

THE SECRET WORLD OF POLLY FLINT
DEAR SHRINK
THE PIEMAKERS
A GAME OF CATCH
THE WINTER OF THE BIRDS
THE BONGLEWEED
THE BEACHCOMBERS
UP THE PIER
THE NIGHT WATCHMEN

The Bagthorpe Saga
ORDINARY JACK
ABSOLUTE ZERO
BAGTHORPES UNLIMITED
BAGTHORPES V. THE WORLD

For Cedric,
Ruth and Oriane Messina,
with love

ONE

The younger Bagthorpes were sitting under a hedge opening their school reports. They had this off to a fine art, and did it on the last day of every term. William would take a camping kettle and stove in his duffel bag and hide them in the undergrowth on the way in to school.

"It's no use slitting the envelopes open and then taping them up afterward," he had told the others. "Even Father's not *that* stupid. We'll have to steam them open properly."

This they accordingly did, and over the years the report-opening ceremony had come to be quite a highlight of their lives, and one that they enjoyed, by and large. With typical Bagthorpian thoroughness they had by now elaborated the thing into a kind of ritual, with rules, and combined it with a feast. Jack, Rosie and Tess would cram *their* bags with various delicacies from the pantry, and bottles of pop.

On this occasion they settled themselves comfortably under the hedge, and began to tuck into the food while they waited for the kettle, filled with water from a nearby stream, to build up a good head of steam.

"I still think we ought to have filled the kettle with fizzy lemonade," Rosie said. "It would've been a scientific experiment."

"In which we would all probably have lost our eyebrows," Tess told her.

"And the envelopes would have smelled of pop," Jack put in, feeling this to be a valid and intelligent point. (He did not often get the chance to be valid and intelligent. He was not a genius, as the rest of them were.)

"Father's got hay fever," Rosie returned. "He can't even smell a peppermint. He said so himself."

William took a well-thumbed notebook out of his pocket. It contained the rules of all kinds of Bagthorpe competitions and games, including this one.

"You to open first," he told Rosie. "Then Tess, then Jack, then me. Who's got the pens?"

"I have," Jack told him, and fished them out of his rucksack.

The pens were crucial to the whole thing. Over the years the Junior Bagthorpes had built up an impressive collection of them, with a widely varying range of nibs and ink colors. They were used to forge a variety of flattering comments about the Bagthorpes' prowess and conduct. They came in handiest at the very end of the reports, where a large blank space was left for the headmaster's remarks.

All too often the headmaster, when faced with the task of commenting on the Bagthorpes, found himself at a loss for words. If he said anything complimentary, he would be perjuring himself. If he gave his honest opinion, Mr. Bagthorpe would be round to the school like a shot, yelling and threatening to write to the Governors of the school and even, on one occasion, his Member of Parliament. As the headmaster saw little likelihood of any remark of his influencing the Bagthorpes' future behavior, he would wisely leave the space blank. This gave them carte blanche to make their own remarks, and they took full advantage of it.

"We've got to be a bit careful this term," William said, as Rosie held her envelope in the now steady jet of steam. "We overdid it a bit, last time."

This was true. Where a teacher had made such a comment as: "Jack's Latin will undoubtedly improve when he learns to conjugate," Tess (who was best at forging handwriting, and also knew the most long words) had added: "He is, however, the most promising student I have ever encountered, and heading, I predict, for a Classics Exhibition in the fullness of time."

More work had to be done on Jack's report than on anyone else's, because he did not have a single good subject. William and Rosie were walking computers and good on the science side, and Tess's languages, especially her French, were better even than her teacher's. The previous terms Tess had had to tinker with virtually every remark made on Jack's report. When it came to maths and science she was temporarily stumped. The master concerned had used green ink, of which she had none. The remarks made, however, were extremely unflattering and could not be allowed to stand.

What Tess had in the end decided on was to add further remarks, in a different-colored ink and different handwriting, followed by fictitious initials.

"Tell them you have two different teachers for maths and the sciences," she told Jack. "Tell them it's a new policy."

The amended report had read as follows:

Arithmetic: Jack's numerical aptitude leaves much to be desired.   M.W.
However, his mathematics show great originality. It must be remembered that Einstein was a late developer.   P.C.

Geometry: Jack's ability in this subject is confined to his occasionally managing to draw straight lines.   M.W.

There are doubtless still new theorems to be discovered, and Jack is all the time pushing out the boundaries in this direction. P.C.

Algebra: Jack seems genuinely puzzled by the combination of the alphabet and numerals. Let us hope that light will eventually dawn. M.W.
When it does, I expect great things from this remarkable pupil. P.C.

Latin: Jack's Latin will undoubtedly improve when he learns to conjugate. *He is, however, the most promising student I have ever encountered, and heading, I predict, for a Classics Exhibition in the fullness of time.* B.R.

French: Jack's progress is slow, and his accent painful. *However, one has the impression of vast latent potential, yet to be unleashed. I look forward to this.* S.G.

English: Jack should aim at a closer relationship with the Oxford English Dictionary so that his spelling falls in line with that of the rest of us.
One has little doubt, however, that he will follow in the footsteps of his distinguished father, and give the nation great things. D.F.

History: Fair. Jack really must try to sort out his Henrys. *This, though, is a minor point. His grasp of the broad sweep of history from the beginnings of recorded time to the present day is astonishing.* C.M.

Geography: Jack still continues to refer to "top and bottom, left and right" instead of North, South, East and West. He may find this unsatisfactory to his eventual Examining Board.

But his general feel for the subject is phenomenal. Reading his recent project on India, one could almost believe that he was a reincarnation of Gandhi. **L.G.**

Physics: Jack must learn not to leap to irrational conclusions. He needs careful watching when conducting experiments. **W.M.**

I hope that he will eventually make a career in nuclear physics, where his true bent lies. E.K.

Art: Jack's work is definitely of the Impressionist School. *So, of course, was that of Monet and Pissarro.* **A.R.**

Biology: Jack does not seem to know what he is doing in dissection. **W.M.**

Far from being a drawback, this enables him to see each experiment with an open outlook and to draw his own conclusions—rather in the manner of Darwin. **E.K.**

P.E.:   Jack's enthusiasm is not, unfortunately, matched by his agility and coordination. He falls over a great deal.

This, of course, is an art in itself, and one mastered only by the world's greatest acrobats and clowns. **G.L.**

Headmaster's
Remarks: *It is a privilege and a delight to my staff to teach yet another gifted scion of the Bagthorpe family. His achievements make us all feel humble. D.N.*

The schizophrenic nature of most of the remarks on this report had considerably confused Mrs. Bagthorpe. On her initial readthrough, she murmured "Oh, dear!" and "Oh, *lovely!*" alternately. After rereading it numerous times in an effort to extract some kind of balanced picture of Jack's progress, she said:

"Oh, well, I expect what they're really saying is that you have ups and downs. Anyway, well done, darling!"

Mr. Bagthorpe had skimmed through it and instantly fastened on the bit about himself.

" 'Distinguished,' eh . . . !" he said. " 'Given great things to the nation . . . .' Perfectly true, of course, though I'm bound to say that *I* hadn't noticed any signs of your following in my footsteps. Few could, of course. And I categorically forbid you to take up a career in nuclear physics. I should like to think that when the end of the world comes, it will be in its own good time, not as a result of you mixing up a couple of buttons and starting a nuclear holocaust."

"I must say *that* bit rather surprised me," Mrs. Bagthorpe had said. "Do you think perhaps I should go to the school and have a word with Jack's science teacher?"

The younger Bagthorpes had exchanged anguished glances and held their breaths. If their mother *did* do this, the result would itself be little less than a nuclear holocaust. Two holocausts, in fact—one at home and the other at school. They had been producing forged school reports for years, and all would inevitably be exposed.

Fortunately, Mrs. Bagthorpe had decided against this course of action.

"Let's wait and see what they say *next* term," she had said sensibly.

The Junior Bagthorpes had been sufficiently scared by this narrow shave to decide that in future they would have to temper their forged remarks to some degree.

"After all," William had pointed out, "there's only Jack

among us who's really dim. The rest of us get fairly good reports anyway."

"Not about your conduct, you don't," Jack had argued. "I get the best conduct."

This was unarguable. His siblings were a sore scourge to the teaching staff of their schools. (Rosie, who was only nine, was still in the Juniors.)

On this occasion it was her report that was first to be doctored. Using Jack's penknife, she carefully eased open the gummy flap of the envelope and extracted the report. She opened it up and the others watched as she read it.

"Ooooh!" she squealed. "It's not true, it's not!"

"What's it say, Rosie?" Jack asked.

"That foul Miss Barton's only *put* it because I keep catching her out on the computer. *I* could teach computers better than she does. She's a real idiot. *And* she wears horrible perfume and stinks the whole classroom up. Some days I can't even think for stink!"

"Yes, but what's she *say*?" Jack persisted.

" 'Rosie continues to make good progress,' " Rosie read out. " 'But she seems to find it difficult to keep in line with the rest of the class. There is no advantage in rushing ahead, and she goes so fast that one rather suspects that she is picking up a superficial knowledge of subjects. This will not serve her well when she reaches a more advanced stage of her schooling. I'm sure you are aware that computer addiction is a very real problem with some children, and I would not wish to see Rosie become such a case.

" 'Her conduct is fair. She must accept that I, and not she, am the head of this class.' "

"Cheek!" exclaimed Tess indignantly. "D'you remember her saying that about *me*, when I was in her class?"

"And me," put in William. "Who's she think she is?"

"Anyway, we've got to put some better things than that!" Rosie said. "I'm *easily* top of the class, by miles and miles. And she hasn't said one single word about my brilliant art and that fantastic clay dinosaur I made."

"Don't worry, Rosie," Tess told her. "Here, give it to me. What sort of pen's she used? Oh, easy. Italic. Easy to forge *her* handwriting. If she does classic italic, and teaches it to everybody she ever has in her class, it serves her right if she gets forged."

"It took me years to get rid of that handwriting," William said. "Handwriting should be individual and reflect the personality of the writer. I'm definitely not an italic personality."

"I think I am," said Jack humbly.

"Well, yes," William said. "I meant the rest of us."

"You be steaming my envelope open, Jack," Tess told him, "while I get going with this. Now, let's see...."

She selected a pen with an italic nib and tried it out on a page of her file.

"Good. Black. Plain sailing."

Tess got to work while the others returned their attention to the food.

"Right," she said at last. "How about this? 'The foregoing remarks reflect only the purely negative side of Rosie's work and behavior. I am bound to redress the balance by saying that I have never, in my entire career, encountered a child with such a command of the computer. It amounts to genius.' "

"That's better!" exclaimed Rosie with satisfaction.

"Shut up!" William told her. "Go on, Tess."

" 'Rosie's brilliance in this field,' " Tess continued, " 'is matched by that in most other subjects. She is a prolific story writer and her projects are exemplary.' "

"What's that mean?" Rosie interrupted.

"Brilliant," William told her. "It's what teachers say instead of brilliant. Sounds better."

"Oh."

"D'you want to hear this, or not?" Tess said. " 'I'm sure I need hardly tell you that Rosie's artwork is that of a prodigy. Her portraits, in particular, are always speaking likenesses, and this term she has also produced a quite outstanding dinosaur in clay.

" 'Rosie is always eager and helpful. I look upon her as my right hand in the class. She is a born leader.' Well—what d'you think?"

"Ace!" said Rosie with satisfaction. "If she'd put all that herself in the first place, there'd be no need for us to go adding it on. Jolly good, Tess. Thanks. Give it back here, and I'll get the envelope stuck down again."

And so the Bagthorpes spent a happy hour consuming their End Of Term Feast and doctoring the reports.

"Better not go over the top when you're doing yours, Tess," William told her.

He usually gave her this warning since the time she used the word "genius" eleven times, and Mrs. Bagthorpe had thought this excessive. She did not, in fact, smell a rat, but simply thought it showed a somewhat limited vocabulary.

"And don't make me out to be so good at maths and physics this time," Jack told her. "Just make me out to be average. I'm not even that, and if I'm not careful, I'll end up doing Advanced Science."

By the time the forgeries were completed and the last crumb of the feast eaten, it was almost lunchtime.

"Hope Fozzy won't have done anything too filling for lunch," Rosie said. "Else I'll bust!"

"She'll be in a bad temper anyway," Jack said. "She always is on the last day of term."

A disinterested party might think Mrs. Fosdyke's bad temper justified on these occasions. She came in on a daily basis to help Mrs. Bagthorpe with the running of the house, but had always refused to live in. This, she had told her cronies in The Fiddler's Arms, would be more than flesh and blood could stand. She felt it would shorten her life.

"The goings on at that house," she told them, time and again, "is unbelievable. Mad as hatters, the lot of them. Especially *him*."

By this she meant Mr. Bagthorpe, with whom she carried on a perpetual feud. She aggravated him at least as much as he aggravated her. Her principal weapon in this guerrilla warfare was the Hoover, with which she rumbled endlessly about the house, making the maximum possible racket in the vicinity of his study, and, he maintained, wearing out the carpets in the process.

"There are no other carpets in England that have to take the kind of stressing she gives mine with that everlasting Hoover," he would say. "Hedgehogging about from morning till night, sucking up invisible fluff and destroying the vibrations in my study. Not even Buckingham Palace gets vacuumed like I do."

Mr. Bagthorpe, then, was the main thorn in Mrs. Fosdyke's flesh, but most of the time his offspring ran him a close second. For one thing they were (with the exception of Jack) perpetually and noisily practicing musical instruments, and for another they were continually getting what she called "under her feet."

During term time Mrs. Fosdyke enjoyed relative peace on

the home front, and saw the younger Bagthorpes only for an hour at the start and end of the day. Holidays, however, were another matter, and their approach always aroused in her dark feelings of gloom and foreboding.

"Seven whole weeks!" she told her cronies despairingly over the froth of her stout. (She drank Guinness stout because she had heard that it was good for the nerves, and she felt that her own nerves suffered such constant wear and tear at Unicorn House that she was in regular need of its medicinal properties.)

"Seven whole weeks of 'em, morning, noon and night!" She shuddered expressively.

"It must be terrible, Glad," said Mrs. Pye sympathetically.

"Don't they ever go away?" inquired Mrs. Bates.

Mrs. Fosdyke shook her head.

"Too mean," she said. "*He* once went to some newfangled Health Farm. Only for a week, though. And only when he'd won it free, that time they was going mad doing competitions and pulling labels off all my tins."

"Pity," said Mrs. Pye. "It'd give you a nice rest, Glad, if only they was to go on holiday."

"That nice Reverend gentleman—brother of Mr. Bagthorpe's, though you'd never think it—'e invited them to go and stop only last month, but he wouldn't. Oh, no. 'E wasn't going to let 'imself in for a diet of nuts and grass, he said. They're vegitarians, you know. Never *touched* my Boeuf Bourguignon last time they was here. I could've wept. And there's another thing, of course. . . ." Here Mrs. Fosdyke lowered her voice and darted her eyes rapidly about, with the air of one who has some dark intelligence to impart.

"What, Glad?" prompted Mrs. Pye in a hoarse whisper.

"Drink. They're teetotal as well, you see. And Mr. Bagthorpe, 'e don't like to be caught too far off of a whisky bottle."

"Alcoholic, is he?" inquired Mrs. Bates with relish.

"I ain't saying that," said Mrs. Fosdyke, piously. (She had lived among the Bagthorpes long enough to be aware of the laws of slander. Mr. Bagthorpe, in particular, was always threatening to invoke them, and she had no wish to be served with a writ.) " 'E just likes 'is little nip, that's all I'm saying."

"Oh." Mrs. Bates sank back, patently disappointed. "P'raps he'll end up as one, anyhow."

"Seven whole weeks!" Mrs. Fosdyke drew a deep breath and was back on her original tack.

When the younger Bagthorpes arrived back at Unicorn House, they were met by a delicious scent of savory steam.

"Steak and kidney pud!" Rosie whispered to Jack. "Just our luck! I *shall* bust!"

As they entered the kitchen, Mrs. Fosdyke glanced unenthusiastically up from the sink.

"Holidays, Mrs. Fosdyke!" said Jack, with an attempt to generate cheerfulness.

"Huh!" Mrs. Fosdyke gave a little disgusted snort. "Holidays for *some*, you mean."

She commenced a great rattling of pans in the sink to underline her point.

"Darlings—you're back!" It was Mrs. Bagthorpe, who, having spent the morning wrestling with the Problems of readers, in her role as Agony Aunt in a monthly column for a woman's journal, had now emerged to face the very real Problem of her own family.

"We've got our reports!" Rosie told her. "Ouch!"

She was kicked sharply on the ankle by Tess, who had

specifically warned her not to mention the reports until one or the other of their parents asked for them.

"People are supposed to *dread* their parents opening their reports," she had told her. "You'll give the whole thing away." "Don't open them until we've had lunch, will you?" Tess now pretended to plead. "I bet they're *terrible!*"

"Oh, Tess, I'm *sure* they're not," replied Mrs. Bagthorpe laughingly, as well she might, given the kind of eulogies she was by now accustomed to. "Are we ready to eat, Mrs. Fosdyke?"

"*I* am," she replied unhelpfully.

"Go and tell the others, Jack," Mrs. Bagthorpe told him.

Jack went out and nearly tripped over Zero. The dog was obviously keeping out of Mrs. Fosdyke's way while there was no one there to stick up for him. She went on a lot about his pawmarks on the floor, and the amount he ate.

"Good boy," Jack told him. "Good old chap. It's holidays now, and we'll go on some fantastic walks. And I'll teach you some new tricks if you like."

Zero moved his tail feebly at this optimistic suggestion. He was not, in fact, very good at picking up tricks. To date, all he could do was fetch sticks and sit up for biscuits. Mr. Bagthorpe said that all other dogs were *born* being able to do both these things. His opinion of Zero's I.Q. and appearance was very low.

"Mutton-headed, pudding-footed hound," was how he described him, mostly. Zero slunk very close to the ground when Mr. Bagthorpe was around, and his ears drooped.

Jack went to his father's study and put his ear to the door to see if there were any sounds that might indicate whether he was in there, creating. (Mr. Bagthorpe wrote scripts for television, and claimed to be sensitive and creative.) Suddenly the door whipped open and Mr. Bagthorpe came charging straight into the listening Jack. He let out a yelp of shock.

"What are you doing?" he demanded. "Why are you listening outside my door? Out of my way!" He strode past Jack and down the hall. "And get your grandmother down here. I want you all down here, sharp!"

Jack peered into the sitting room and saw Grandpa watching television with a look of beatific peace that was strangely out of place in such a household.

"Lunch, Grandpa!" Jack shouted into his hearing aid.

Grandpa nodded and beamed. He was the least trouble of anyone in the family, and was protected from a lot of the yelling that went on by his deafness. Uncle Parker said that, like many other deaf people, Grandpa was only S.D.—Selectively Deaf. This meant that he heard only what he wanted to hear.

Grandma, Jack thought ruefully as he climbed the stairs to her room, was another can of worms entirely. Her chief interest in life was stirring up rows, especially with her son. She would go to great lengths and do a lot of plotting to achieve a really good row. She left Lucrezia Borgia, as Mr. Bagthorpe often pointed out, standing.

"This looks like being her lucky day," Jack thought.

TWO

Mr. Bagthorpe had felt a nervous breakdown coming on for months—possibly even years. When his jars of homemade wine and beer had exploded with all the random violence of a terrorist gun raid, he had taken the whole thing personally.

"I am a marked man," he declared. "There is no place for me in nature."

"I have often thought the same, Henry," remarked Grandma, "but had never thought to hear you admit it."

"You, Mother, brought me into this world," he told her, "and it is a mystery to me why, having done so, you appear to devote every waking moment to making my existence purgatory."

"I have never wished for anything but your happiness, Henry," said Grandma piously and with a fine disregard for accuracy. "And I did, if you remember, warn you against the practice of brewing intoxicating liquors. You are scarcely able to brew a pot of tea without incident."

"Let us forget all about the whole thing," interceded Mrs. Bagthorpe brightly. "It was a very interesting experiment in Self-Sufficiency, Henry, and terribly clever of you to think of it. But I think we must put the whole thing behind us. Put it down to experience."

"It was certainly that," said William with feeling. "Do I, by any chance, *resemble* a beet root?"

He was referring to the diet of unparalleled monotony and charmlessness to which the entire menage had been condemned by Mr. Bagthorpe's ill-fated venture into Self-Sufficiency. This had consisted mainly of variations on a theme of beet root, spring onions and rhubarb. Mrs. Fosdyke, indeed, had very nearly handed in her notice at this time. Had she in fact done so, Mr. Bagthorpe at least would have felt that the end had justified the means.

As it was, the explosion of his wines had marked the end of Self-Sufficiency and the Bagthorpes had gradually lapsed into their old ways. The period of relative calm that followed did not suit Mr. Bagthorpe at all. The peacefulness made him edgy.

He had decided, therefore, to announce his nervous breakdown, and a little plan that he had been privately hatching. He sat, glaring, at the head of the table while Mrs. Fosdyke and his wife clattered about serving up the lunch. He couldn't stand noise. He thought that any noise was aimed at him personally. (In Mrs. Fosdyke's case, of course, it often was.)

Grandma was the last to arrive and took her own place at the table, looking distinctly pleased with herself.

"I have sent off for my horoscope to be read," she told the table at large.

This remark would have fallen on deaf ears in the normal run of things. The Bagthorpes never allowed conversation to get in the way of their food. On this occasion, however, an end of term picnic had been eaten only an hour earlier, and anticipation of steak and kidney pudding was not running high.

"You don't believe *that* bilge, Grandma, surely?" said William.

"Your grandmother," Mr. Bagthorpe told him, "believes in any bilge that is going, and always has. And all that Breathing she goes in for has only worsened her condition." (Grandma and Mrs. Bagthorpe had both taken up Yoga some time before.)

"I have had to give the exact moment of my birth," Grandma went on, ignoring him. "This is apparently most important. Fortunately, my dear mother kept a journal. The entry for that day says, 'Dear little Grace born at 3:17 A.M. Thanks to the Lord for this blessing.' "

"At that stage, of course, she had no way of knowing what she was stuck with," said Mr. Bagthorpe. "And haven't you left it rather late in life to start investigating your fate in the stars?"

"I find that kind of remark very hurtful, Henry," she told him. "One day, you will be old yourself."

This gave Mr. Bagthorpe the cue he had been waiting for. The dishing up was complete, everybody was now seated, and his stage was set.

"On the contrary, Mother," he said, "I shall *not* be old myself. There is no way, living in this household, that I shall reach my allotted span. You all sit here, calmly forking up steak and kidney, and not one single one of you has noticed the condition I am in."

Mrs. Bagthorpe looked up at this.

"Why, Henry?" she inquired. "What condition *are* you in?"

"Laura," he said, "I am having a nervous breakdown."

"But you're *always* having them, Father," Rosie piped up. "You can't expect us to notice *every* time you get one. Don't you want to see our reports? Ouch!"

She was rewarded for this latter remark by another savage kick on the ankle from Tess, who sensed that the present atmosphere was not conducive to opening reports, however good.

"Reports!" Mr. Bagthorpe threw down his knife and fork. "Here I am, in the grip of a severe, suicidal—"

"Why do you not consult the doctor, Henry?" interrupted Grandma. "No one should attempt diagnosis of their own condition."

"I do not need that half-baked quack to tell me whether or not I am having a nervous breakdown. He could not diagnose whooping cough at five yards. He couldn't diagnose *leprosy*."

"Then what *do* you intend to do about it, Henry?" inquired his wife. "And what do you wish *us* to do about it?"

"Fortunately," he replied, "I expect nothing from any of you. I have learned to expect nothing. I have made my own arrangements."

"Like what?" said William.

"I have decided," said Mr. Bagthorpe, "that what I need is a change. I am cooped up in this godforsaken household day in day out, year in year out, surrounded by everlasting racket" —here he cast a baleful look toward Mrs. Fosdyke—"and can go on no longer. What I need"—here he paused for effect— "is a holiday."

He was not disappointed by the reaction. This statement brought a gratifying response. Mrs. Fosdyke, indeed, actually choked. She spluttered so convulsively that she created quite a diversion. Mr. Bagthorpe, believing that she was faking this paroxysm to draw interest away from himself and his announcement, fixed her with a murderous glare. (In this he was mistaken. Mrs. Fosdyke had a cousin who had died choking on a well-known brand of breakfast cereal, and understandably did not wish to go the same way.)

"Did you say a *holiday*?" Tess said disbelievingly, when Mrs. Bagthorpe had finished thumping Mrs. Fosdyke's back.

"But we *never* go on holidays," said Rosie.

"Will it be Abroad?" asked William hopefully. He had won several gallons of a suntan oil during the Competition-Entering days, and thought it might at last come in useful, English weather making very few demands on it.

"It most certainly will be Abroad," Mr. Bagthorpe replied. Now, at last, he had the stunned silence he had hoped for. The whole table stared at him in utter disbelief. They had been treated, over the years, to endless monologues on the subject of "Abroad."

To say that Mr. Bagthorpe did not care for Abroad would be a serious understatement. He dismissed the entire world outside his own native country as if it were the lowest circle of Dante's Hell. He had tried it, he told his family, and found it wanting.

In the first place, foreigners did not speak English. "If the language of Shakespeare and Milton is good enough for us," he would say, "it's good enough for them." They also had a regrettable tendency to "overdo the garlic." It was almost impossible, once Abroad, to find any decent reading matter. Anything available was either in a foreign language or a third-rate whodunit, and all too often both. He did not care for everlasting sunshine, believing it to be weakening for the character. He had no wish to lie on a beach all day oiled like a sardine and with approximately as much turning space. The only concession he would grant was that the drink was cheap.

"And even that's no comfort," he would say, "given the amount of it you have to drink in order to forget that you are Abroad."

Given all this, then, it was not surprising that his family was rendered temporarily speechless by the intelligence that they were to go for a holiday Abroad. Rosie, who as youngest had heard fewer of Mr. Bagthorpe's diatribes than the rest, was the first to speak.

"Oh, yippee, Father! Ace! Are we going to Majorca?"

It was now Mr. Bagthorpe's turn to choke. In his book, some Abroads were worse than others, and rock bottom, so far as he was concerned, was Majorca.

"It is full of bookies' windows, the overspill from Blackpool and fish-and-chip shops," was his often repeated verdict on this island paradise. "And mad black-haired women throwing themselves about, clacking castanets at you."

All present were now watching Mr. Bagthorpe, who had tears gushing from his eyes as a result of the string bean lodged in his throat. As they sat and waited for him to reveal his choice of location Abroad, there was the unmistakable shriek of brakes and sound of tires spinning on gravel that heralded the arrival of Uncle Parker.

Mr. Bagthorpe attempted to curse through the obstacle of string bean, failed, and choked the more.

"Oooh—I hope Daisy's brought Billy Goat Gruff!" Rosie cried, pushing back her chair.

"You ain't ate much," observed Mrs. Fosdyke sourly. "And I don't want no goats in *my* kitchen, thank you."

"Hello, all!" Uncle Parker breezed in with his customary carefree style. He was followed closely by Aunt Celia, who looked rather as if she were going to a fancy dress party as a waterfall, and their daughter. Daisy Parker was only five years old, but could create more havoc, Mr. Bagthorpe maintained, than a fully paid-up member of the Mafia.

On this occasion she came trotting in holding a long length of pink satin ribbon on the end of which was a goat. Round its neck were wound further furbelows of ribbons and bells, and judging by its baleful gaze it did not feel comfortable in these.

"I brought Billy Goat Gruff!" squealed that awesome child. "He's come to play with Little Tommy and Zero. Where's Zero, Zack?"

"Under the table," Jack told her. "I don't think you ought to go mixing the goat with him and Little Tommy, Daisy. Look what happened at your Banquet."

At the Parkers' Banquet, a combination of goat, dogs and Grandma's cat, Thomas the Second, had resulted in the total demolition of the Parkers' dining room (including the chandeliers) and in several people being bitten.

Mrs. Fosdyke let out a disgusted snort, got up from the table and started banging pots and pans about as only she knew how.

"That woman bangs pots like she was being paid a fiver per decibel," Mr. Bagthorpe would say.

"Had some bad news, Henry?" inquired Uncle Parker, surveying Mr. Bagthorpe's scarlet and tear-stained face. "Bad luck. One of your scripts get turned down?"

"He was just going to tell us where we're going for a holiday," Jack told him, "but he started choking."

"We're going *Abroad*," added Rosie.

"Holiday?" echoed Uncle Parker. "*Abroad?* By Jove, Henry, *this* is something of a turnabout."

"A rose red city, half as old as time . . . ," murmured Aunt Celia. "Magic casements . . . perilous seas in faery lands forlorn . . . ."

The rest of the Bagthorpes looked askance at this utterance, though they were well used to Aunt Celia, if she spoke at all, doing so in rhyming couplets or blank verse. She sank into a deep chair, probably overcome by the strong fumes of steak and kidney. (Aunt Celia was a vegetarian, and rarely did more than toy with lettuce at mealtimes.)

"Going on *holidays!*" squealed Daisy. "Oooh—can *I* come?"

This optimistic request produced a further fit of choking from Mr. Bagthorpe.

"And Billy Goat Gruff! Can *he* come? He goes everywhere wiv me, he even goes to *bed* wiv me!"

Jack was surprised to hear this, given that the goat was not, so far as he knew, house-trained. He supposed that the Parkers were so relieved that Daisy was not at present setting fire to everything, or making floods, that the goat, however messy, provided a welcome alternative.

"We shall have to see," said Uncle Parker, with intent to infuriate. "What do you say, Henry?"

Mr. Bagthorpe could not, of course, say anything, wrestling as he was with the errant string bean lodged in his windpipe.

"Of course darling Daisy can come, too," Grandma answered on his behalf. "Though I am not so sure about the dear goat. I believe there are rather stringent quarantine laws about taking animals Abroad. I expect I shall have to leave my own darling Thomas the Second behind."

And Zero, thought Jack. His heart sank. This had only just occurred to him. Who'll look after him? Not *Fozzy.* . . . And he *can't* go to kennels—it'd kill him. I'll have to stop behind with him.

While Jack was making this noble resolution, the goat, evidently rendered nervous by the presence of so many Bagthorpes, made a remarkably large puddle on the floor.

"Oooh!" squealed Daisy. "You *naughty* Billy! I *told* you not to do vat. I told you *millions* of times!"

Mr. Bagthorpe, who could hear, even if he could not speak, was temporarily cheered by this remark. It meant, he thought with satisfaction, that during the goat's residence with the Parkers he must have made regular and numerous such puddles, and that by now the whole house must pretty well reek of goat.

He was alone in being pleased by this event. Jack saw Mrs. Fosdyke throw up her hands in a shower of suds and roll her eyes toward heaven. He could actually see the whites of her eyes, and wondered for a moment if she had finally been driven mad. She was always claiming to be on the verge of this.

Mrs. Bagthorpe rose and went to search for something to mop up the goat's misdemeanor.

"Take Billy out, why don't you?" Uncle Parker suggested. "Let him have a wander round the garden and see if he can find something to eat."

Mrs. Bagthorpe pursed her lips at this. She was a keen gardener, and knew from experience that the goat would head straight for her most succulent cuttings.

"He likes paper best," Daisy demurred. "A'n't you got no paper? Uncle Bag's got *lots* of paper, I seen it!"

"Unfortunately, Daisy," said Uncle Parker, "Henry puts an unaccountably high value on any paper on which he has written."

At this, Mr. Bagthorpe's choking began to look as if it might be terminal.

"I'll come with you, Daisy," Rosie offered. She alone of the Bagthorpes, with the exception of Grandma, really liked Daisy, and thought her truly sweet.

Daisy shook her head.

"No fanks!" she said decisively. "Me and Billy Goat Gruff wants to do somefing secret."

This was, of course, a highly ominous remark, coming from Daisy. Had the Bagthorpes been less taken up by the astonishing prospect of a holiday Abroad, they would have been alerted by it. Someone would have been deputed to keep a strict eye on her. As it was, Daisy and her satin-swathed goat went trotting and tinkling off into the garden unattended.

"Well, Henry," said Uncle Parker cheerfully, "what's it all about? Holiday abroad, eh?"

Mr. Bagthorpe had finished choking but was all the same still rendered speechless by fury. The pleasure he had anticipated in making his announcement of his plans had been destroyed at a stroke by Uncle Parker's advent. He had set his stage beautifully, had the whole family gazing at him, breath held, and now he had lost them. No one was paying him proper attention.

"You, of course," he told Uncle Parker, "do not need holidays. Your entire existence is a nonstop holiday—filling in crosswords, swigging gin and tonic by the—"

"Well, yes," admitted Uncle Parker affably. "I do take things fairly easily, by and large. Unlike yourself, Henry."

"Henry has no aptitude for leisure," Grandma said. "To be able to enjoy leisure is a fruit of the civilized man. Henry, unfortunately, is *un*civilized."

"Thank you, Mother," said Mr. Bagthorpe.

"Oh, come *on*, Father!" cried Rosie impatiently. "Get *on* with it! Where are we going?"

"Very well," said Mr. Bagthorpe. He paused. "We are going—to Wales!"

There was a short, but pregnant, pause, and then all present let rip. Some hooted, others protested, one rolled up her eyes again. Aunt Celia carried on gazing into space as she so often did, Grandpa carried on with his steak and kidney, oblivious to everything, and Uncle Parker smiled.

The smile was slight—a mere *hint* of amusement combined

with a tinge of superiority. Unlike Mr. Bagthorpe, he never overplayed his hand. He went in for understatement, and that, in a family that went in for so much hyperbole, was an ace card.

Mr. Bagthorpe saw that smile, and was duly maddened by it. Tess's cry, "Abroad—Wales isn't Abroad!," William's "Bang goes any chance of needing suntan oil," Rosie's "Aren't we even going on an airplane, then?" all went unheeded. Mr. Bagthorpe was aware only of the ever so slight smile of Uncle Parker.

He opened his mouth, intending to emit a bellow that would effectively quieten the whole assembly.

"A-shoo!" The sneeze was of an impressive order, and followed by another of equal force. "A-shoo!"

Mr. Bagthorpe's eyes were streaming again.

"There!" exclaimed his wife triumphantly. "I *knew* your hay fever was all in the mind!"

"Don't talk such—shoo!"

Mr. Bagthorpe and his wife often had rows about his hay fever. She maintained that he had had his worst attack on their honeymoon, in Venice, when there was not a blade of grass to be seen, let alone hay.

"There are no hayfields in Venice," she would declare, "no wheat and no corn. There are not even any gardens—only window boxes. There is only yourself, Henry, who could claim to have been given hay fever by a window box."

Mr. Bagthorpe, for whatever cause, was now sneezing violently, nonstop, while the rest argued and complained.

"I do not think that we should discuss this now!" said Mrs. Bagthorpe loudly, at last. This directive went unheard. You had to raise your voice very loudly indeed to have any chance of being heard at Unicorn House.

"Stop!" she then shrieked. "Be quiet, this minute!"

Mrs. Bagthorpe did not, as a rule, believe in raising her voice, which was a very unyogic thing to do. All present were sufficiently impressed that she should now do so, to stop dead in their respective tracks.

"A-shoo! A-shoo!" Mr. Bagthorpe sneezed desperately in the ensuing silence.

"We will go into the whole matter later, when Henry has calmed down," Mrs. Bagthorpe told them.

"Which'll be never," muttered William, sotto voce.

"Can we do the reports now?" asked Rosie. "And don't dare kick me again, Tess."

"I should like to hear more about this holiday," said Grandma, who rarely fell in with other people's wishes if she could help it.

At this point Mr. Bagthorpe's sneezing fit miraculously subsided.

"There is no need for you to hear about it," he told her, "because you will not be going."

Mr. Bagthorpe was wearing a smile of grim satisfaction. He was more or less certain that he had her now.

What had in fact happened was that, as Uncle Parker had so uncannily divined, Mr. Bagthorpe had had one of his scripts turned down. Nobody knew this but himself, because if it were generally known, it would become ammunition for use against him by his unfeeling relatives.

He had noticed that ghost stories were currently much in vogue, so had turned his hand to writing one himself, comforting himself for this apparent comedown (he usually wrote socially relevant scripts) by reflecting that even Shakespeare was not above deploying the odd ghost. His script had been duly returned with the comment that although the general idea was good, it was lacking in what the script editor called "authentic atmosphere." He had jokingly added, "Perhaps you should try living in a haunted house."

Mr. Bagthorpe had taken this suggestion with absolute seriousness. He had immediately put an advertisement in several papers and journals:

> Required for six weeks from mid-July large family house sleep six. Must be haunted No unhaunted houses need apply.

He had had several replies to this advertisement, and had selected as most promising a house in mid-Wales which had, its owner claimed, not one but several ghosts. Mr. Bagthorpe had already taken this, and paid in advance.

He was particularly pleased with his scheme. It would combine a holiday with serious research, which he could then set against taxes. Also—and this he considered to be a master stroke—it would automatically exclude Grandma, who was frightened of ghosts.

Now, therefore, his smile broadened.

"I am rather interested in Wales, myself," Grandma went on, "and I am pleased that we shall not be going anywhere in an airplane. I do not care for them, and nor do I believe in the statistics. They are constantly crashing."

"You will not be coming, Mother," repeated Mr. Bagthorpe.

"Henry, dear—" Mrs. Bagthorpe started to protest, although she herself welcomed the prospect of a few weeks away from Grandma.

"And the reason you will not be going," he continued, "is that I have taken a house that is haunted."

The response to this intelligence was gratifying, and a moderate babble set up among his offspring.

"It is haunted," he added for good measure, "not by a single ghost, but by several, I am informed."

"You took the house," said Grandma frigidly, "with the express intention of excluding myself from a much needed holiday with my dear family."

"On the contrary, Mother, I took it in the interests of research," he told her, neglecting to mention his rejected script. "I am engaged in writing a very difficult and complex piece, and can get no further with it until I have had firsthand acquaintance with a haunting."

He paused, and looked about him at his now attentive relatives.

"We must hope," he added, "that you lot will not have the effect of frightening the ghosts off."

"We'll be able to tell when the ghosts are there by Zero," said Jack. He alone had been pleased to hear that Abroad was to be Wales. Now, not only could Zero accompany the family, but he would have an important and unique role to play.

"Dogs have got sixth sense," he explained, seeing the blank faces of the rest. "Their fur stands up on end when they see ghosts. That'll be really interesting, seeing Zero's fur stand up on end."

"Sixth sense?" echoed Mr. Bagthorpe disgustedly. "That numb-skulled hound hasn't even got the normal quota of senses, for heaven's sake. And if his fur's going to stand on end, you'd better get it unmatted, quick."

"Well," drawled Uncle Parker, "you are nothing if not original, Henry. Where exactly in Wales is this phantom-infested pile?"

"Oh, I don't know," Mr. Bagthorpe replied offhandedly.

This was true. He never troubled to consult maps. "Somewhere beginning with a double L, I expect. Ha!"

"I'll be able to do some research as well," Tess said. She was currently very interested in the paranormal, and had several experiments going, involving seeds, razor blades and dead mice.

"Do you think you have a phobia about ghosts, Grandma?" she asked.

"Henry knows this perfectly well," said Grandma coldly. "I do not believe a word of what he says. He has never researched anything in his life. Right from boyhood, if he has not known anything he has simply made it up as he went along."

"Well, there's no need to worry," Tess assured her. "I have a manual of hypnotism. Phobias are quite easily cured by hypnotic suggestion. I shall cure you before we go, Grandma."

"Thank you, dear child," replied Grandma. "There, you see, Henry. I *shall* be going, despite your nefarious plotting."

"Can you *really* hypnotize, Tess?" asked Rosie with awe.

"Of course she can't," said William jealously. "She's just trying to get another String to her Bow, to outdo me."

"On the contrary," replied Tess calmly, "yesterday I hypnotized Philip Robinson to a very deep level."

"So what did you hypnotize him to do?" asked William. "Cough up his pocket money?"

"I think you are confusing serious hypnotism with cheap stage acts," Tess told him. "As a matter of fact, I was going to regress him to an earlier incarnation, but unfortunately the bell went."

"You haven't left him sitting there hypnotized for the whole holiday, I hope," said William.

"Reincarnation?" exclaimed Grandma. "How very interesting. When you have cured me of my phobia about ghosts, I would like you to regress myself, Tess. It will be fascinating to discover who I was in my previous existences."

"The Marquis de Sade, for one, I shouldn't wonder," said Mr. Bagthorpe.

"'As everybody finished?" demanded Mrs. Fosdyke, who was not interested in philosophical debate. "Because there's treacle sponge yet."

"Certainly, Mrs. Fosdyke," said Mrs. Bagthorpe, grateful for the interruption. "Let me help you. Pass Grandpa's plate, William, and—" She broke off in mid-sentence.

There came a series of loud bangs and crashes, mixed in with screams and wailing.

"Daisy!" said William, pushing back his chair. "Come on, everyone, quick, or she'll have the whole place ablaze!"

"*Now* what?" With a despairing cry Mrs. Fosdyke plonked her pudding on the draining board and made for the door. The treacle sponge slid gracefully off the plate and into the sink.

THREE

The events of the next few minutes were so complicated and fast moving that afterward none of them could really remember them very clearly. (This did not, of course, prevent them from inventing their own versions, and passing them off as fact.)

The Bagthorpes rushed out of the kitchen to find china and furniture being smashed at an unprecedented rate.

"Oooh!" screamed Mrs. Fosdyke, vainly trying to dart in several directions at once to field the flying china. "Oooh, me Rockingham, ooh, me Wedgwood!"

"Oh, Billy Billy Billy!" squealed Daisy, rushing hither and thither. "What's the matter with my poor little Billy?"

She was alone in her concern for the goat's health and well-being, though it had, to judge by its behavior, gone berserk. It was reeling from side to side, charging at everything in its path and hiccupping violently. Daisy was scampering after it, trying to catch hold of its satin ribbons, and herself doing almost as much damage as the goat in the process.

"Oooh!" she squealed, as she tripped over a wire and sent a lamp crashing onto an ormolu clock which would never strike again.

"Stop 'im!" shrieked Mrs. Fosdyke. "Stop 'im!"

Nobody obeyed this instruction. The goat's behavior was so bizarre that they were frightened. Nobody wished to be bitten.

"There!" exclaimed Mr. Bagthorpe with satisfaction. "*Now*

you see the animal in its true light!" (Mr. Bagthorpe had had an earlier encounter with the goat in which it had, he claimed, tried to kill him.)

The Bagthorpes stood helplessly watching the devastation of their sitting room, keeping near to the door in case they had to run. Then, before their astonished eyes, the goat made one last plunge that brought down the curtains, rail and all, and slumped in a heap to the floor.

A stunned silence followed.

"Oooeeh!" Daisy let out a long, high wail. "Oh, my darling little Billy, oh, he's dead, he's dead!"

She ran over and started disentangling his bells and ribbons from the curtains. The others advanced somewhat more slowly. The animal did indeed appear to be dead, but they were taking no chances. They advanced rather as if they were playing "What Time Is It, Mr. Wolf?" or "Grandmother's Footsteps."

"It could just be lying doggo," said Mr. Bagthorpe, voicing everyone else's fears, "ready to get up, and charge again. That goat's a killer."

The goat did not, however, get up. When they finally reached it, they could see that it was not dead, as they had hoped, but appeared to be in a deep, peaceful sleep, breathing heavily and letting out an occasional hiccup.

"Oh, dear!" said Mrs. Bagthorpe weakly, looking about her at the wreckage.

"Oh, darling little Billy," sobbed Daisy. "He *i'n't* dead, he's jus' asleep."

"Don't cry, Daisy darling," Grandma told her. "All's well that ends well."

"Well?" echoed Mr. Bagthorpe. "*Well?* You should take

up writing slogans, Mother, for the politicians. You sound like a politician summing up the Wall Street Crash. Someone get that accursed infant and her unholy goat out of here and off the premises. I am going to my study, and I am not to be disturbed."

He left the room and crossed the hall to his study. They heard first the door opening and then, almost immediately, a terrible cry of rage and despair. He came hurtling back into the sitting room.

"They've been in there!" he yelled. "That infernal goat's been eating my papers!"

"Perhaps that's what's wrong with him," suggested Jack, in what he hoped was a helpful way. "Perhaps he's just got indigestion."

At this juncture Uncle Parker appeared on the scene. He had probably stayed behind in the kitchen to calm Aunt Celia, who was easily unhinged.

"What's up?" he inquired pleasantly. "Hello, Daisy. What's with the goat?"

"I fink he's jus' tired, Daddy," she replied. "He been very busy."

The others were still reeling before this understated description of the goat's recent activity when Mrs. Fosdyke was heard saying:

"What's that 'orrible smell? There's all my furniture and china smashed to smithereens and now there's a smell all over everywhere. Where's it from?"

At first the Bagthorpes had difficulty in locating the source of this query. They then spotted her emerging on hands and knees from beneath the tangled drapes. She knelt for a moment, sniffing noisily.

Up to this point everybody had been too distracted to do much sniffing. Now they followed Mrs. Fosdyke's example, and found that there was, indeed, a strong smell.

"Scotch!" exclaimed Mr. Bagthorpe. "It's Scotch!"

The goat hiccupped and emitted a long snore. The Bagthorpes stared at it, light dawning.

Billy Goat Gruff was drunk.

Later that day, in accordance with Bagthorpe tradition, a thoroughgoing inquest was held into the day's events. This was considerably hampered by the fact that the chief witness, namely Daisy, was missing. She had been borne away by Aunt Celia, who was wailing, "Oh, my darling Daisy, why do you persecute her so?"

Uncle Parker had bundled his wife and daughter into the car and driven off at speed with them and the still unconscious goat. Mr. Bagthorpe gave him enough time to reach home, and then embarked on a series of long and increasingly noisy telephone calls to him. They were noisy, at any rate, at the Bagthorpe end of the line.

A reconstruction of the movements of Daisy and Billy Goat Gruff that afternoon, after they had left the house, ran as follows.

Daisy had gone into the garden as Uncle Parker suggested, but apparently with no real intention of staying out there. One of Daisy's many worrying traits was that of extreme stubbornness. She never allowed herself to be deflected from her purpose. Once an idea entered her head, she pursued it with ruthless determination to its final, and all too often fatal, conclusion. On this occasion she had got it into her head that Billy Goat Gruff wanted some paper to eat.

This commodity being in short supply on the grounds of Unicorn House, Daisy had first led the goat to Mrs. Bagthorpe's newly transplanted cuttings and, when he had polished off these, back to the house in search of his second course.

She was sufficiently wily not to re-enter by the kitchen door. Daisy might or might not be a genius, as Aunt Celia claimed, but she was certainly very wily indeed for a five-year-old.

"Come on, Billy Goat Gruff," she urged her charge, "let's go in froo vese uvver doors and get some of Uncle Bag's paper."

The pair of them had accordingly re-entered the house by the French doors, which were standing open on account of the warm weather. Once in Mr. Bagthorpe's study, which he had incautiously left unlocked (as a result, he later maintained, of being thrown off balance by finding Jack with his ear to the door), Daisy had fed the goat various pieces of paper from the desk.

Billy Goat Gruff had not, fortunately, been very hungry by now, and had consumed mercifully few items. One of these, however, was a check for a sum running into four figures, a rebate from the Inland Revenue. This had hit Mr. Bagthorpe particularly hard, as he had been counting on this sum to finance the holiday in Wales, which he would then claim *back* from the Inland Revenue.

"And it'll be the year A.D. 2000 before they replace it," he told his family bitterly. "It was two years overdue as it was."

He was tempted to tell Uncle Parker that the goat had devoured his latest script, and put in a claim for loss of earnings. In the end, foreseeing that it might then emerge that the script had in fact been turned down, he decided against this misrepresentation.

Apparently when the goat had fed he was in the habit of

downing a quantity of water, and Daisy had conscientiously tried to provide a substitute for this. She heard the commotion coming from the kitchen and had wisely decided not to return there. Instead, she had trotted across to the sitting room, poured a large measure of whisky into a Wedgwood ashtray, and placed it before her pet.

He had lapped it up with such speed that Daisy replenished the ashtray with another liberal dose of Scotch, and so on until the goat had reached an advanced stage of intoxication. He had then blown his mind, and set about the destruction of the sitting room with a thoroughness that the Bagthorpes had themselves witnessed.

So, unfortunately, had Mrs. Fosdyke. As soon as the Parkers had driven off, she announced that she had a serious headache, probably the worst she had ever had in her life. She then went home, leaving all the washing up.

"This 'eadache might not've gone by tomorrow," she had warned before she departed. "Nor the day after, come to that. That Daisy Parker should've been put down at birth."

Mr. Bagthorpe, reluctant as he was to side with Mrs. Fosdyke about anything, was inclined to agree with her on this point. He did not, however, say so.

"There is little doubt that her headaches, unlike my own crippling bouts of hay fever, are all in the mind," he contented himself with observing. "With any luck, she'll hand in her notice."

Nobody else agreed. They were all extremely bad tempered at the prospect of spending the rest of the day clearing up the wreckage, though Rosie's devotion to Daisy was such that she made excuses for her, even while assisting in this task.

"Father shouldn't leave whisky bottles lying about where

there are young children," she said. "Alcohol's a poison, Aunt Penelope says so."

"Do not bother quoting your Aunt Penelope to me," Mr. Bagthorpe told her, and went to make another of his phone calls to Uncle Parker.

"How was poor little Daisy to know not to give it to Billy Goat Gruff?" Rosie continued. "And what if she'd drunk some herself? It could have *killed* her."

The rest of the clearing-up squad (which did not, naturally, include Grandma) were as one in thinking that this would have been a welcome eventuality. Daisy's popularity rating in the Bagthorpe household, never high, was now running at an all-time low.

"They haven't even looked at our reports," William said. "We might as well not have bothered."

"*I* might not, you mean," Tess corrected him. "All *you* do is bask in the reflected glory."

The bickering went on all afternoon. The state of the sitting room was such that the task before them seemed hopeless.

"It's like cleansing the Augean stables," Tess said glumly. "It always is, when Daisy's been here."

Mrs. Bagthorpe went out for the afternoon, in her capacity as a Justice of the Peace.

"Though I don't expect anyone so depraved as that offspring of Russell and Celia's will be brought before the bench," Mr. Bagthorpe told her.

"On my return, Henry, I shall want to have a serious word with you," she responded. "Concerning this so-called holiday that you have arranged without consulting myself."

"Oh? Why? *You* frightened of ghosts as well, are you? I should have credited you with more sense."

38

"I shall not discuss it now," she told him, and left.

The younger Bagthorpes overheard this exchange, and the prospect of a row between their parents cheered them at least a little.

By evening most of the smashed china had been swept up, the curtains were rehung and the dismantled furniture lay in neat piles. On her return from Aysham, Mrs. Bagthorpe, who seemed in better humor than when she had left (possibly because she had had a few hours' rest from her family), inspected the scene of the disaster and praised her offspring for their efforts.

"Well done!" she exclaimed. "What is for supper?"

They all looked blank.

"Mrs. Fosdyke, you remember, went home," she reminded them.

The young Bagthorpes gloomily investigated the contents of the deep freeze, opened a giant can of beans, laid the table and assembled round it. They picked half-heartedly at their food and waited for the row to begin. They were not disappointed.

Mr. Bagthorpe unwittingly gave his wife an early cue.

"What's this?" he demanded, eyeing his plate with distaste. "These sausages are still pink. We shall all die of salmonella."

"Precisely, Henry," said Mrs. Bagthorpe.

"What do you mean, precisely?" he expostulated. "Why are we being made to eat this muck?"

"Your memory is remarkably short, dear," she replied. "Mrs. Fosdyke is not with us."

"Amen to that!" he said, pushing his pink sausage to one side and chasing his baked beans.

"That remark is hardly logical," she said. "You cannot have your cake and eat it."

"And on this occasion—neither!" he replied. "Ha!"

"But at any rate," she continued, "your rather childish attitude is leading directly to the matter I wish to discuss with you."

"You are not on the bench now, Laura," he returned, "and that nannyish tone does not become you."

The younger Bagthorpes were perking up by the minute. The confrontation was developing very promisingly.

"I am referring, of course," she went on, "to that extraordinary announcement you made at lunchtime."

"Pray do not trouble on my behalf, Laura," Grandma interposed, hoping to add fuel to the flames. "Henry's malicious plot has been foiled. I am having my first hypnotic session with dear Tess directly after supper."

"Any chance of putting her in a trance and leaving her there?" Mr. Bagthorpe asked.

"You will not evade the issue by flippancy," Mrs. Bagthorpe told him. "And the issue is not whether or not we shall be accompanied by Mother. It is whether or not we shall be accompanied by Mrs. Fosdyke."

Silence. Mr. Bagthorpe boggled. His jaw dropped.

"Mrs.—?" His voice was strangled. "Have you gone *mad*, Laura?"

"No, Henry, I have not. When you were planning your holiday, you did not, I suppose, give a single thought to myself?"

"Of course I didn't," he agreed. "Why should I?"

"Because I, too, am a breadwinner in this household," she returned, "and at least as much in need of a holiday as yourself."

"But you're *going*!" he expostulated. "What on earth are you talking about?"

"I will put the matter plainly," she said.

"You do that," he told her.

"It is not my idea of a holiday, Henry, to be cooped up in a large house in mid-Wales with all the cleaning, washing, ironing, cooking—"

"There's no need to labor the point," he told her. "I get your drift. You will *not* be doing all those things. We shall have a rota."

"In the past," she told him coldly, "you have successfully managed to remove *yourself* from any rota within hours of its being drawn up."

"He deliberately sucks things up the Hoover and jams it," Rosie piped up. "*And* shrinks things on purpose in the washing machine, and makes all the colors run. My vests are still green from the last time."

"*And* always burns things," William put in. "He's hopeless at cooking. And all *I* can do is bacon and egg."

"I'm not much good, either," Jack said. "I honestly think we ought to take Fozzy, Father."

"Hear, hear!" chorused his siblings. Because of their fondness for food they were forced into an ambivalent attitude toward Mrs. Fosdyke. They were prepared to suffer her presence, however unattractive, because of the outstanding quality of her cuisine. Mrs. Fosdyke could have been a Cordon Bleu if she had ever heard of such a thing.

"I never complain," said Grandma inaccurately, "but I do not think I could face food of this order over an extended period."

"There!" said Mrs. Bagthorpe. "You see? Everyone agrees with me. Mrs. Fosdyke will go."

"Mrs. Fosdyke will not go," he returned calmly. "The house only sleeps six."

Mrs. Bagthorpe glowered down the table at him, faced with this apparent impasse.

"Well, eight at a pinch," he conceded. "But if Mother and Father are now going, that would leave Fozzy camping on the grounds. I do not see Mrs. Fosdyke in a tent."

Nor did anyone else. His family tittered unfeelingly at the picture this conjured up. Mrs. Fosdyke, who wore fur-edged slippers winter and summer alike to "keep off the cramps," was by no means the outdoor type.

"Very well!" Mrs. Bagthorpe drew a deep breath. "In that case, *I* shall not go, either."

All eyes now turned on her.

"It will be a holiday in itself for me to have a few weeks on my own," she continued. "In fact, I look forward to the prospect."

"But who'll do the cooking?" wailed Rosie.

"I don't mind sleeping in a tent," said Jack helpfully. "In fact, me and Zero'd like it."

"Leaving *me* to share a room with Fozzy, I suppose?" said William with heavy sarcasm.

"There is, I suppose, a further possibility," Mrs. Bagthorpe said. "You could telephone, Henry, and see if there is a room in the village that Mrs. Fosdyke might have. She might even prefer such an arrangement."

Mrs. Bagthorpe had never said a truer word. If she had been able to hear what Mrs. Fosdyke was at that very moment saying to her cronies in The Fiddler's Arms, she would not have been optimistic about making any arrangements at all for her to accompany the family to Wales.

Mrs. Fosdyke, whose nerves had been severely strained by the day's events, was by now on her third stout, and well into her stride.

"I've told you time and again, it's no use me trying to describe it," she told her attentive audience. "There's nobody who hasn't been through it could ever understand. It's like having a baby, or the atomic bomb."

"We did see a *bit* of the goings on, Glad," Mrs. Pye reminded her. "The time that Daisy made a flood, and wetted all the beds, and that."

"That," said Mrs. Fosdyke decisively, "was *nothing*, Flo." (This was not what she had said at the time.) "If you could've seen that mad goat ramming my furniture, and tossing hairlooms into bits and—his eyes was all red, you know, just like in them films!"

"Oooh—'orrible!" Her friends shuddered sympathetically.

"Drank pints and pints of whisky, he had," continued Mrs. Fosdyke, "and for two pins, I'd report that Daisy Parker to the R.S.P.C.A."

"Oooh, yes, why don't you?" cried Mrs. Bates encouragingly.

"Because, Flo, they'd all gang up on me," replied Mrs. Fosdyke. "They'd make out that goat was never drunk at all, and where'd that leave me? Next thing I knew, I'd be had up for perjury."

Her audience could see that this would, indeed, leave Mrs. Fosdyke in a difficult position, and said so. It was in fact true that the Bagthorpe clan, however bloody their internal feuds, would by unspoken agreement stick together if threatened by an outsider.

"Any'ow, this stout 'as 'elped my 'eadache a bit," Mrs. Fosdyke said. "I'll 'ave another, I think, else I don't suppose I'll sleep a wink tonight."

Mrs. Pye, hoping for further revelations, obligingly replenished her glass.

"But fancy them going on holiday, Glad," she prompted, "after all you was saying the other night. You must be psychic."

"I think I am, a bit," agreed Mrs. Fosdyke modestly.

"And abroad!" put in Mrs. Bates.

Mrs. Fosdyke snorted.

"Wales!" she said disgustedly. "*That* ain't proper Abroad! You 'ave to go in a airplane to go proper Abroad."

"Like Ireland," supplied Mrs. Pye.

"And what was that you was saying about ghosts, and hauntings?" inquired Mrs. Bates.

"That's 'is cunningness," Mrs. Fosdyke explained. " 'E's ever so cunning, for all 'e's as mad as a hatter. It's 'is way of stopping Mrs. Bagthorpe Senior going with 'em. She's a bad old woman, that I'll admit, and thick as thieves with that Daisy Parker, but she is 'is own mother, and blood's thicker than water, or should be."

The trio sat nodding sagely over this incontrovertible truth.

"There's one thing, Glad," said Mrs. Bates at length. "If they're all going off to Wales, it'll at least give your nerves a rest."

"Oooh, it *will!*" said Mrs. Fosdyke with feeling. "I can't 'ardly believe it. Six 'ole weeks without that lot under my feet morning, noon and night. I still can't 'ardly believe my luck!"

Mrs. Fosdyke was right to suspend her belief. In her experience, nothing even remotely connected with the Bagthorpes had brought her any luck, and nor would it now.

She took a long, enjoyable gulp of her stout, and thought herself in very heaven. She really should have known better.

FOUR

The relief of Mrs. Fosdyke's headache by her Guinness was only temporary, and she took the next day off.

That'll give 'em time to get that room to rights, she reflected, not that it ever will be, of course. I used to fair enjoy dusting in there. Nothing much left to dust now, I s'pose. And if them alcoholic fumes 'as got into the furnishings, it'll smell for everlasting of a gin palace.

Her employer's mood was not noticeably more cheerful. Mrs. Bagthorpe's Yoga and deep breathing helped her to cope with ordinary, run-of-the-mill stresses, but let her down on occasions such as yesterday. She had been in a fair lather over her husband's holiday plans, when there was still the goat to come.

She did, however, try to Think Positively, and was also fairly (though not outstandingly) sensible by nature.

"If a situation is worrying you," she told herself firmly, "it is best to take Positive Steps to rectify matters. Take the bull by the horns."

The bull in this case being Mr. Bagthorpe, she requested the telephone number of the man who had rented him the house in Wales. At first he refused.

"His name's Jones," he told her. "Look him up in the telephone directory. Ha!"

In the end he gave in and Mrs. Bagthorpe made her call.

"That's splendid," she told the others, who had assembled in the kitchen for a mid-morning snack, breakfast having been uneatable. "Mr. Jones says that there is a small cottage on the grounds nearby that will be exactly the thing for Mrs. Fosdyke."

"And how much is *that* going to cost?" demanded Mr. Bagthorpe. "You said a room, Laura. Now it's a cottage that—"

"The rent is extremely reasonable," she told him. "So much so, in fact, that I thought I had misheard him, and asked him to repeat it. The figure is no higher than one would expect to pay for a single room. *I* shall pay it, Henry. I do not want our holiday spoiled by your sulking over such a petty detail."

There were only four days to go before they left for Wales, and everybody set about assembling the things they wished to take with them. This included a large number of musical instruments. William played the drums, Rosie the violin and cello and Tess the oboe and piano (though she had been dissuaded from attempting to pack the latter). William was speculating about the viability of dismantling his radio mast in the garden, and taking that.

"There are a lot of mountains in Wales," he said, "which will interfere with radio waves. And I don't want to risk losing some of my contacts. Especially Anonymous from Grimsby."

Grandma dispatched Jack to the village shop with a request for as many as possible large, empty cartons. When he took these up to her, he found the room almost unrecognizable.

"Gosh, Grandma," said Jack, "it's completely bare! I don't honestly think there'll be another Burglary, you know. Lightning never strikes in the same place twice."

This, coming from a member of the Bagthorpe family, was rich. At their house, lightning was apt to strike not twice, but with regularity and at frequent intervals.

"I cannot exist for six weeks without my dearest possessions," Grandma told him. "My room is my solace and my sanctuary, where I can retire to escape the hurly-burly of everyday life."

Considering that Grandma was herself responsible for much of the hurly-burly at Unicorn House, and indeed appeared to thrive on it, this struck Jack as strange.

"But you're not taking that lot *with* you, are you? I thought you were just packing them up out of the way of burglars."

"I shall not set foot out of this house without them," she replied.

When Mr. Bagthorpe saw the mounting heap of luggage in the hall, he immediately ordered everybody to take their stuff back to their rooms and unpack it.

"It would take a fleet of cars to move that stuff," he said, "and I am not Paul Getty."

Mrs. Bagthorpe intervened.

"I have been thinking, Henry," she said. "There are nine of us to be transported, and naturally quite a lot of luggage. I think that we should hire a minibus."

"At the rate this lot are going, a furniture removal van would be more appropriate," he returned.

"Don't be silly, Henry," she told him, and went off to order a minibus.

As soon as this news reached the rest of the family, they all immediately upped their quantity of luggage. Even Grandpa had a large pile of fishing gear and a portable television set.

Mrs. Bagthorpe went down to the village to inquire after Mrs. Fosdyke's headache, and invite her to accompany them to Wales. This invitation Mrs. Fosdyke at first pretended to refuse, and at last accepted with a great show of reluctance.

This, given Mrs. Fosdyke's earlier pronouncements in The Fiddler's Arms, might strike some people as inconsistent. The truth of the matter, however, was that Mrs. Fosdyke was at least as dependent on the Bagthorpes as they were on her. After only a few days away from them, she would find herself oddly out of sorts and restless. A comparison might be made between this and the withdrawal symptoms suffered by a drug addict. When people were in the vicinity of the Bagthorpes, their adrenalin tended to flow. Mrs. Fosdyke was no exception. Her adrenalin glands were in a constant state of arousal; she was kept on a permanent "high." She would never, even under torture, have admitted to *liking* the Bagthorpes. She was simply addicted to them.

Had she been required to live under the same roof for six weeks, she might have decided against the venture. But the prospect of having her own private cottage appealed to her greatly.

"At least I can 'ave nice quiet evenings," she told herself naively.

Having accepted the invitation and returned to her duties at Unicorn House, Mrs. Fosdyke became very bossy. She instantly set about ordering large quantities of groceries and provisions from the village shop.

"But, Mrs. Fosdyke," protested Mrs. Bagthorpe, eyeing dubiously the tall towers and pyramids of packets and cans, "surely we can purchase all these commodities when we get there?"

"We're going Abroad, don't forget," said Mrs. Fosdyke darkly. "I ain't getting stuck anywhere foreign with all kinds of packets on shelves you can't read a word of, and brands you've never heard of, and—"

"But we are only going to Wales," Mrs. Bagthorpe said weakly. "I'm sure we'll find—"

"My sister in Portsmouth once brought me back a cake mix from Majorca," Mrs. Fosdyke rambled on regardless, "and I could make neither head nor tail of it. All them foreign instructions. And I ain't sure I should have fancied it, anyhow. Threw it in the bin, in the end. 'Ave you taken out some Insurance?"

"Insurance?" echoed Mrs. Bagthorpe, temporarily thrown by this abrupt change of tack.

"People that goes Abroad usually takes out Insurance," said Mrs. Fosdyke lugubriously. "My sister in Portsmouth always does. *And* tablets from the doctor in case your tummy goes off. *Not*, of course, that there'll be anything wrong with *my* cooking. *I* shan't go lathering everything in olive oil. But it's the water you've got to be careful about, see. I think you ought to take out some Insurance, Mrs. Bagthorpe, I do really."

It was fortunate that Mr. Bagthorpe was not around to hear this, the topic of insurance being a highly inflammatory one at the present time. He had already had several very embarrassing telephone conversations with the insurance people over the havoc wreaked by Daisy and her goat. He had been asked to describe the whole incident in writing, and was finding this extremely difficult.

"It reads like a script for the Marx Brothers," he told the others, "or a missing last act from *King Lear*. I doubt whether any insurance inspector in England will be able to take such a claim seriously. They'll never believe it. When I see it put down in black and white, even *I* don't believe it. And when the premium goes up again, Russell will have to foot the bill. If he'd invested in a good psychiatrist years ago for that unhinged daughter of his, it would have worked out cheaper for everybody in the long run."

During those days of preparation for the expedition, there

were numerous phone calls to Unicorn House, mainly from Daisy Parker, and for either Rosie or Grandma. These were the only two people in the Bagthorpe menage who liked and sympathized with Daisy.

"Keep asking Uncle Bag if I can come," she begged them. "Ask 'n' ask 'n' ask him. Me and Billy Goat Gruff want to go to Wales. There's *dragons* in Wales, Mummy says so."

"That," said Mr. Bagthorpe when he was told of this, "is exactly the kind of half-baked notion with which Celia has been cramming that brat's head since she was born. She is now reaping her just rewards."

"Nonsense, Henry," Grandma said. "You have not an ounce of poetry in your soul. I see no reason at all why Daisy should not accompany us. She would take up very little room."

"Room?" echoed Mr. Bagthorpe. "*Room?* England, Europe, the world, the entire universe would not contain—"

"Do not trouble launching into one of your exaggerated tirades," Grandma told him. "Daisy is just a normal, high-spirited five-year-old, though admittedly unusually creative."

"And black," gritted Mr. Bagthorpe, "is white!"

Despite sustained canvassing on Daisy's behalf by both Rosie and Grandma, she was not to be allowed to accompany the party. Jack himself was relieved.

Most dragons breathe fire, he thought, and if Daisy thinks Wales is full of dragons, that means she's back into her Fire Phase.

Also, he thought Daisy herself a sufficiently formidable personality to frighten off any ghosts. This would infuriate Mr. Bagthorpe, who was hoping to establish contact with them, and disappoint both Tess and himself. Jack was not conducting any paranormal experiments, as she was; he was just curious. He also wanted to get Rosie to photograph Zero with his fur standing up on end.

The day of the departure dawned bright and sunny and this seemed (mistakenly, as it turned out) to augur well for their holiday. At eight o'clock the minibus arrived. They had made arrangements for it to convey themselves and their luggage to Wales, and then collect them in six weeks' time. Mrs. Bagthorpe would follow the bus in convoy, driving the family estate car, to carry excess baggage, and for use while they were away.

"We do not wish to be cut off entirely from civilization!" Mrs. Bagthorpe had laughingly remarked. Most people acquainted with the Bagthorpes would have said that they were at a fair remove from civilization for most of the time.

"Look, squire," the bus driver said to Mr. Bagthorpe when he saw the mountain of luggage assembled in the drive. "This is a minibus, not a bleeding removal van."

"We are taking only the barest minimum," Mr. Bagthorpe lied acidly.

At that moment there came the sound of spurting gravel. The Parkers had come to make their farewells.

"My word, Henry," said Uncle Parker, eyeing the Everest of luggage, "it is easy to see that *your* lot don't travel with only a toothbrush."

Daisy, with Billy Goat Gruff in tow on a long yellow ribbon, began to sob heartily.

"One of the things we have to look forward to in the coming weeks, Russell," said Mr. Bagthorpe, "is a respite from the attentions of your deranged daughter. Why have you brought that goat back onto my premises?"

"The goat's only crime," replied Uncle Parker, "was to down one Scotch too many. I should have thought you could have sympathized with that, Henry."

"Wales . . . ever-singing Wales . . . .," murmured Aunt Celia. She was wearing her waterfall outfit again.

"Yes, dearest, yes," said Uncle Parker. "Though it'll have less to sing about when this lot take up residence."

"Uncle Bag's nasty," sobbed Daisy. "Now I shan't *never* see no dragons."

"Look, Daisy," said her father, "pretend Billy Goat Gruff's a dragon, why don't you?"

" 'Cos he 'an't got no fire," sobbed Daisy. "Dragons got *fire!*"

Hearing this, Jack again mentally congratulated his father on his decision to leave Daisy on English soil.

It was a two-hour job to fit the Bagthorpes' minimum of belongings into the two vehicles. Twice everything was nearly stowed, and then had to be taken out again, and a new start made.

"Rather like one of those executive desk puzzles," drawled Uncle Parker. "Any executive who could solve this one would deserve to be made chairman of British Rail tomorrow. Not," he added, "that *their* record with luggage is unspotted."

The bus driver put the matter more succinctly.

"It's like trying to get a bleeding gallon into a pint pot," he said.

"The expression is 'quart,' " Mr. Bagthorpe told him coldly. "A quart into a pint pot."

"Look, squire," said the driver, "I *said* gallon, and I *meant* bleeding gallon."

During this arduous two hours Daisy eventually cheered

up and, along with Billy Goat Gruff, managed to amuse herself. Nobody had been detailed to watch her movements. This was a pity, as they were later to discover.

At last the Bagthorpes and their belongings were crammed into the two vehicles.

"You're sure that's the lot?" inquired the driver. "Not forgotten the lawn mower, or the piano?"

"Drive on!" Mr. Bagthorpe told him curtly.

He had elected to travel in the minibus rather than with his wife, partly because anyone who traveled with the latter would do so with fishing rods waving past his ear, and partly because he suspected that Grandma would hatch plots against him if he were not there.

In the end, nobody wanted to sit with Mrs. Bagthorpe.

"But I shall have no one to talk to," she protested.

"Then it will give you a chance to think your own thoughts," her husband told her. "It's to be hoped they don't send you to sleep at the wheel—ha!"

Jack gave the driver instructions for reaching Mrs. Fosdyke's house in Passingham, and by the time they arrived all the passengers (with the exception of Grandma) were well into a noisy rendering of "We'll Keep a Welcome," which alerted the neighbors and ensured a watching pair of eyes behind every net curtain.

Mrs. Fosdyke emerged wearing her best peach crepe two piece and a matching hat with half veil. She gave the impression that she was expecting to be personally greeted by the Prince and Princess of Wales on crossing the border, and Mr. Bagthorpe said as much.

"You're late," she said accusingly as she mounted the steps. "Been sat waiting near on two hour, I have."

Jack, picturing her sitting expectantly, fully packed, on the edge of a chair in her kitchen, all dressed up, let out a smothered laugh. She gave him a sharp look but nonetheless elected to sit next to him. (The choice was not wide. The only other remaining seat was next to Mr. Bagthorpe himself.)

"At least you, lady, 'aven't brought your three-piece suite along with you," said the driver, hauling up her one suitcase, lavishly festooned with labels bearing the legend WALES in bright red capitals.

"Quite a bit of the stuff in the back's hers," Jack told him, in the interests of fairness. The minibus was so well provisioned that, had it been cut off in an unseasonable blizzard, its occupants could have survived for a month.

Once Mrs. Fosdyke and her luggage were installed, Mrs. Bagthorpe pipped merrily on her hooter from the rear, and the expedition was under way.

The minibus driver had probably never had such noisy passengers, even those bound for football matches. The Bagthorpes had a long and well-loved list of car games that they always played on journeys. These involved a great deal of shrieking, hooting, arguing and, in Grandma's case, cheating.

"You can't 'ardly 'ear yourself drive," Jack heard the driver mutter under his breath. After a time, thinking it only polite, Jack asked him if he would like to join in.

"No thanks, son," was the reply. "I've got enough on trying to concentrate on the road as it is."

Frequent stops in towns were made for Grandma, who had a weak bladder, or at any rate said she had. On these occasions the rest of the party scattered at speed and disappeared into various shops. The driver then had great difficulty in reassembling his passengers.

On the last of these stops he said to Grandma, "Look, lady, this is the last town. We're over the Welsh border in a couple of miles, and from then on, it'll have to be hedges."

At this Grandma fixed him with a quelling look, and the rest guffawed.

"Over the Welsh border, did you say?" asked Mrs. Fosdyke nervously. Then, to Jack, "Are you *sure* we don't need passports?"

As the boundary line was crossed, the whole party, with the exception of Mrs. Fosdyke, let out a rousing cheer and burst into another chorus of "We'll Keep a Welcome."

"Are *they* Welsh, d'you think?" whispered Mrs. Fosdyke to Jack, prodding him and pointing at a group of walkers with haversacks and woolly hats.

He wondered what Mrs. Fosdyke thought the Welsh ought to look like.

She probably expects them to be barefoot, he thought, and wearing animal skins. Or waving spears with rings through their noses.

Once they were well and truly into Wales, the party became more subdued. They stopped playing games, and instead looked out of the windows at the rolling hills, the rocks and falling streams. There were few signs of human habitation. The farther they went, the wilder and more deserted the landscape.

At present rock climbing and cross-country trekking were Strings to nobody's Bows, but it began to look as if they soon would be.

"You really do not do things by halves, Henry," said Grandma, who was evidently having much the same thoughts. "I had expected scenery, but nothing so drastic as this. I have brought no walking shoes. I do not see myself in flat heels."

"I was just thinking the same, Mrs. Bagthorpe, dear," said Mrs. Fosdyke.

Mr. Bagthorpe glowered at them. Neither was included in the party at his own wish, and now here they were complaining already. Also, he himself didn't care much for the look of the terrain they were now traversing, though he would have died rather than admit this.

"People who cannot adjust should not travel abroad," he told them. "We can always make inquiries about trains back."

Then all at once the landscape became greener and softer, and they found themselves descending into a small, wooded valley with a cluster of houses at the foot.

"Here we are, then!" said the driver. "Llosilly ahead!"

As they drove through the main street, the Bagthorpes noted with relief that there seemed to be several shops. At home, they all made regular forays to the village for extra rations and so on.

The driver drew up and asked a woman the way to *Ty Cilion Duon*.

Mrs. Fosdyke poked Jack yet again.

"*That* one spoke English, at any rate!" she hissed.

The minibus reached the end of the village and entered a wide stone gateway. There it drove up a dark, heavily wooded and overgrown drive and drew up finally in front of a large, gray stone house. The driver switched off the engine. There was a little silence, followed by the sound of Mrs. Bagthorpe's car also drawing up.

"This seems to be it, squire," said the driver. "Rather you than me."

FIVE

The Bagthorpes, as they disembarked, were unusually quiet. They climbed from the warm and womblike shelter of the bus and stood uncertainly as rain spattered from the overhanging trees. They were not used to feelings of strangeness and isolation. They were a match for anyone or anything when they were on home ground, but seemed to have lost at a stroke much of their customary confidence—not to say bombast.

This could not, of course, last for long, nor did it.

"Well, darlings!" It was Mrs. Bagthorpe, advancing toward them in a style reminiscent of Ceres welcoming back Proserpina from the underworld. "Isn't this all splendid?"

At present none of the family felt that they could truthfully agree with this, so no one bothered to reply. Zero seemed the only one glad to be there, and he shot off into the undergrowth.

" 'Taint one bit how I imagined," Mrs. Fosdyke said in a small voice. "And it don't half strike cold. *Degrees* colder it is than in England."

Jack could not help feeling sorry for her. She, too, was off home territory, miles away from everything familiar, and at the mercy of the Bagthorpes. He hoped that she had not forgotten to pack her fur-edged slippers. He suspected that Welsh cramps would be of a more serious order than English ones.

"Where are we going to unload this lot, squire?" the driver asked, mercifully interrupting the party's depressing thoughts with a problem of a practical nature. Mr. Bagthorpe fished about, tried several keys on a large ring, and found the one that fitted. The door swung open with a long, heavy creaking, in the best tradition of the horror movie. Mrs. Fosdyke, who was a keen devotee of this genre, let out an apprehensive gasp. She had up until now been dismissive of Mr. Bagthorpe's claim that the house was haunted, genuinely believing this to have been merely a ploy to put Grandma off coming. Grandma herself looked distinctly nervous as the creaks and groans reverberated about the echoing stone hall beyond. She had undergone a crash course of hypnotherapy with Tess, but was now not sure whether it had worked.

"Right!" said Mr. Bagthorpe, who, as instigator of this present expedition, evidently felt it incumbent on him to take the lead. "Let's get this lot moved. All hands to the wheel!" (Mr. Bagthorpe was not very strong on nautical expressions.)

The next half hour was filled with noisy activity, and by the end of it the Bagthorpes were feeling more or less themselves again. It took a good deal to subdue the Bagthorpes, especially as a clan. Grandma first released Thomas the Second from his basket and the cat, too, skidded off into the undergrowth. She then, having pointed out her own boxes to Jack, and told him to take special care with them, went and sat in Mrs. Bagthorpe's car with her eyes shut. She was probably Breathing. Grandpa, however, trotted back and forth gamely enough, with face alight at the thought of the fishing trips to come.

By the time the minibus drove off, the shadows were lengthening. It had been a long, hard day, and it was not yet over.

"I'm ravenous!" said Rosie, and now that they had time to think about it, they all were.

"Best see where the kitchen is," said Mrs. Fosdyke. "It's to be hoped it's equipped proper."

She advanced across the shadowy, flagstoned hall, an unlikely figure in her peach crepe. She opened a door and peered in.

"*That* ain't it," she said. "Don't look much of a room of *any* sorts, to me."

The Bagthorpes, ever curious, started opening doors themselves. The rooms seemed to share a certain stark simplicity, being all curtainless and uncarpeted and with a minimum of furniture.

"Here we are!" William called. "Here's the kitchen—I think."

They all crowded in through the doorway, allowing Mrs. Fosdyke, as cook, to go first. She took a series of little faltering steps till she was right in the middle of the large room. There she stood looking about her in a genuine daze.

She had done a little secret fantasizing about what her new kitchen might be like, and had looked forward to exploring it and all its different gadgets. She had not gone into exact detail, but had a vague fancy that there would be a lot of stripped pine and stainless steel, like the advertisements on the telly. Also, of course, there would be a Welsh dresser with rows of blue china, and perhaps a jug of marigolds, and a huge, open fireplace, gleaming with brass and copper.

The gap between dream and reality was of such awesome proportions that Mrs. Fosdyke was rendered temporarily speechless. Her mouth made little opening and shutting movements, and her eyes bulged with horrified disbelief. She looked rather like a frog. The Bagthorpes watched her, aghast.

There were only two items in the room that seemed to indicate that this was, indeed, the kitchen. One was a small pottery sink with a single tap, the other a rusty black range of such size and antiquity that it could easily, as Mr. Bagthorpe later said, have been raised from the boiler room of the *Titanic*.

There was a very long silence.

"Oh, dear," murmured Mrs. Bagthorpe at length, "what a dreadful disappointment!"

"This? My kitchen?" Mrs. Fosdyke was in a world of her own now, and speaking her thoughts out loud. She did this a lot at home, after particularly trying days with the Bagthorpes, and found it therapeutic. On this occasion, she had forgotten, presumably, that she had an audience.

"Where's my cooker? Where's my fridge? Where's my working tops?"

The words came out dull and heavy with a measured rhythm, like a sort of desperate poetry.

"All this way we've come, all this way, and now this! I can't believe it, I can't! They're mad as hatters, the lot of them, and now I'm stuck here with 'em for six whole weeks. Six whole weeks! With no cooker, no fridge, no working surfaces, no—"

"It *is* a disappointment," interrupted Mrs. Bagthorpe, fearing that Mrs. Fosdyke was chanting herself into a trance. "And I am so sorry."

"*Nor* hot water, it don't look like," went on Mrs. Fosdyke. "Look at that sink, look at the state it's in. I told 'er we should get some Insurance and tablets from the doctor, but oh, no. . . ."

The Bagthorpes let Mrs. Fosdyke get on with it and rounded, to a man, on the person responsible for the nightmare situation they found themselves in.

"Really, Henry!" expostulated Mrs. Bagthorpe. "Did you not *ask* this Mr. Jones about the amenities?"

Mr. Bagthorpe, who had made no inquiries at all beyond establishing that there were frequent sightings of ghosts, tried to bluster his way out.

"Look, Laura," he told her, "I am a sensitive, creative writer. It is not in my makeup to quibble about trifling domestic details. How was I to know that the kitchen would not measure up to your extravagant expectations? *All* properties these days have modern kitchens."

"Except this one," said William bitterly.

"It is to be hoped," put in Grandma, "that the bathroom arrangements are not equally primitive."

At this, the Bagthorpes scattered to investigate the other amenities. These proved to be few. The furniture in the downstairs rooms amounted to little more than the odd table or chest, and a few deckchairs. The uncarpeted stairs led up to four large bedrooms, in each case containing two bedsteads and nothing else, not even curtains. There was a bathroom of such dilapidation and with such an acreage of worm-eaten mahogany that it must, Mr. Bagthorpe said, have been the first ever installed in the whole of Great Britain, a museum piece of plumbing.

"It ought to have a plaque on it," he said.

However, on the plus side, the house did have electricity and cold running water.

"At least that is a comfort," said Mrs. Bagthorpe, with a feeble attempt to Think Positively. "Think how dreadful it would have been if there weren't either!"

The rest looked at her unsmilingly. Nobody wished to contemplate any such thing. This was one of the many occasions when they were all extremely irritated by Mrs. Bagthorpe's determination to look on the bright side. Only Zero seemed at home. He tore madly around the house after them, raising clouds of dust.

"Perhaps he can already scent ghosts, Father," Jack said.

"That dog," replied Mr. Bagthorpe more or less mechanically, "couldn't sniff a mutton bone at five yards."

"Will we go straight home tomorrow?" Rosie asked.

"We shall not stir from this place," Mr. Bagthorpe replied grimly, "until (a) I have seen a ghost and (b) I have cornered this Mr. Jones and got my money back."

Both these ends, as it turned out, were to be equally hard to achieve.

The family drifted dismally back to the kitchen, where Mrs. Fosdyke was still standing in exactly the same spot, shaking her head.

"Why don't we go and find your little cottage?" suggested Mrs. Bagthorpe brightly. "It's on the grounds quite nearby, Mr. Jones said."

She sounded considerably more optimistic than she felt. She remembered with a sinking heart how surprised she had been at the extreme reasonableness of the rent asked by Mr. Jones. It was possible, she thought, that the amenities of Mrs. Fosdyke's holiday home were as poor as those at *Ty Cilion Duon*.

Here Mrs. Bagthorpe was wrong. The amenities were worse. At first the party went straight past the place, not noticing it behind all the elder and nettles. Anything further removed from Mrs. Fosdyke's mental picture of a bijou, rosebedecked cottage (possibly thatched) could hardly be imagined. It had no electricity, one cold tap and an outside privy. It was also lacking a full complement of roof tiles, and had poison ivy growing in both rooms.

Mrs. Fosdyke had a further turn and had to be led away.

When they got back to the house, Grandma was sitting in a deckchair in what they took to be the sitting room (though there were very few clues to go by), watching Grandpa tinkering with the portable TV set. It was emitting a steady, high-pitched whine and showing a heavy snowstorm.

That's Grandpa's way of escaping from reality, Jack thought. I don't blame him. I hope he gets it working.

"Where is Henry?" Mrs. Bagthorpe asked.

"He said that he would clean up the kitchen," Grandma replied. "Though I must say I thought the offer very uncharacteristic. He is feeling guilt and remorse, I suppose, at having led his innocent family into hell."

"Oh, hardly *hell*, Mother," protested Mrs. Bagthorpe. "In some ways, this might all turn out to be a good thing!"

"In *what* way, exactly, Laura?" inquired Grandma. "Perhaps you will enlighten us all."

"It will bring out our pioneering spirit!" responded Mrs. Bagthorpe. "It is a challenge. We must rise to it."

Her voice trailed off as she surveyed her sullen and dispirited brood. They could rise to a challenge, all right, if occasion demanded. But they preferred to make their own challenges, not have them thrust upon them. They were also very, very hungry, and could see no prospect of a meal in the foreseeable future.

When they entered the kitchen, they were met with a cloud of dust. Mr. Bagthorpe usually let off his feelings by making long and savage phone calls. On this occasion there was no telephone to hand, and so he had been forced into an alternative activity. Hearing his family's coughing and choking, he stopped sweeping and threw down the brush.

"That's better!" he said, presumably meaning the way he felt rather than the state of the room. He had been attacking the dust, rather than steering it in any particular direction, such as out through the back door. The dust had merely been rearranged.

Mrs. Fosdyke let out a little anguished moan.

"Jack, dear, take Mrs. Fosdyke through to the sitting room and put up a deckchair for her," Mrs. Bagthorpe told him hastily. Mrs. Fosdyke was clearly in shock. "We'll bring through some hot, sweet tea directly!" she called after them.

"Using what?" inquired her husband. "I mean, what for a kettle, and what to heat it with?"

Jack returned.

"As a matter of fact," he said, "*I've* got a kettle and stove."

This announcement produced a gratifying response from his audience.

"I thought me and Zero might do a bit of camping," he explained. "So I brought all my stuff. I've got a saucepan and frying pan, as well. And a tin opener and knives and forks, and so on."

"Hurray!" yelled Rosie. "Good old Jack! You're a genius!"

"He is certainly brighter than we have so far given him credit for being," Tess conceded.

"Fish them out, quick!" William told him.

There was a general commotion as Jack raked through the heap of luggage in the hall and retrieved his camping gear, while the others rummaged through Mrs. Fosdyke's Portable Pantry. Under normal circumstances she would never have allowed this, but at present she was sitting on a deckchair looking straight ahead into space.

The promise of food improved everybody's spirits. They got up a menu of bacon, sausage, eggs (rendered during transit suitable for use only as omelettes), followed by tinned apricots. Jack set up the stove, which was fortunately a double one, and soon the kettle was boiling. It was not until this point that they realized that although they could now produce food and drink, they were short of the crockery and cutlery necessary in order for them to consume it. Jack's camping kit provided these commodities for only four persons.

"Never mind," said Mrs. Bagthorpe. "We must have two sittings."

She dispatched Jack with mugs of tea for the occupants of the alleged sitting room, while the others started arguing about who should eat first. They proposed tossing for it, but were forestalled by their mother.

"Your grandparents, Mrs. Fosdyke and myself will be in the first sitting," she said firmly, "and then you children."

"And me," added Mr. Bagthorpe jealously.

"No, Henry, *not* you. There are only *four* of everything, remember. You are the odd one out."

At this Mr. Bagthorpe embarked on a long and bitter speech to the effect that he had always been the odd one out, all his life long, and especially in his own family. Most of this was mercifully lost in the general commotion as his relatives occupied themselves with the meal. On this occasion, too many cooks certainly spoiled the broth for some, in that the heartless younger Bagthorpes served the first sitting extremely anemic-looking bacon and sausage, in order to speed up the arrival of their own (well-frizzled) helpings.

Mr. Bagthorpe himself came in for the underdone meal by virtue of Mrs. Fosdyke's flatly refusing it. She couldn't eat a thing, she said, and didn't feel as if she ever could again. She sat hunched in her deckchair, all the jauntiness lent by her peach crepe having fled entirely. Her whole being seemed shrunken and shriveled. She sat comatose, and allowed arrangements to be made about her as meekly and uninterestedly as if she were a small child.

"Mrs. Fosdyke will share a room with myself tonight," Mrs. Bagthorpe told her husband. "The cottage is quite uninhabitable."

"Rubbish, Laura!" he snapped. "Has she no talent for improvisation? She is exaggerating, of course. She always does."

"Perhaps, then, you would like to sleep there yourself, dear?" said Mrs. Bagthorpe sweetly.

"Right! Right! I will!" Mr. Bagthorpe found it hard to resist any challenge, but on this occasion, of course, he had not yet realized its full extent. When he did see Mrs. Fosdyke's holiday cottage, he was to regret having been so hasty.

The younger Bagthorpes, who *had* seen the outside privy, the half-tiled roof and the poison ivy, tittered into their bacon and eggs.

"Will there be ghosts in there, too, do you think, Father?" asked Tess.

"We'll make notes for you on any we see," William promised. "Clanking chains and all."

"You'd better get your flash equipment ready," Jack told Rosie. "In case Zero's fur stands up on end."

"Cease your idle prattle," Mr. Bagthorpe told them. "I am engaged in a deadly serious piece of creative work. If there are no ghosts, then I shall sue Jones under the Trades Descriptions Act."

The rest of the evening was spent organizing the sleeping arrangements. This was not made easier by there being few electric light bulbs in working order. Grandma requested that she should have one of these in her own room.

"It is not *I* who hanker after an encounter with the spirit world," she said. "I am not even sure that I believe in ghosts. Tess, dear, could we have another session, please, before I retire?"

"Hypnotism doesn't wear *off*, you know, Grandma," Tess told her crossly. "Not on ordinary people, anyhow. You just might not be a very good subject."

Jack himself was rather impressed by Tess's hypnotic powers. He had eavesdropped on a couple of her sessions with Grandma, and had thought he felt himself going under, even without benefit of gazing at her swinging pendulum. His own eyelids had gone heavy after only a minute or so, and he had had to make a real effort to jerk himself back to consciousness. He knew it was important to do this. If he were found in a trance, Tess might make all kinds of unscrupulous suggestions to him.

Like giving her my pocket money, he thought. Bet that's what she'd have done to Philip Robinson, if the bell hadn't gone.

By eleven o'clock the household was ready to settle. Mr. Bagthorpe went lurching out into the darkness, clutching sleeping bag, torch and a recent copy of *Psychic News*. The others waited for a time, half expecting him to come back once he had taken a good look at his squat. To their surprise, this did not happen. Mr. Bagthorpe hated discomfort, but what he hated even more was losing face.

Mrs. Bagthorpe gave him ten minutes, then drew the bolts.

"There is nothing in here your father can possibly want during the night," she told her children, "and so there is no need for us to risk our all being murdered in our beds."

Her offspring were rather alarmed by this unusually strong talk. It made it sound as if she had some sort of inside information.

"Why?" demanded Rosie. "What are the statistics for murder in Wales?"

"Oh, darling!" cried her mother, smitten with remorse. "The statistics are perfectly acceptable. No more murders are committed in Wales than anywhere else."

After this, she laid on the sweetness and light even more heavily than usual. (And this despite the fact that she was genuinely worried about Mrs. Fosdyke's condition. She was in such a zombielike, apathetic state that Mrs. Bagthorpe even feared, at one point, that she might herself have to undress her and put her to bed.)

At all events, Mrs. Bagthorpe rather overcompensated for her earlier remark, and at lights out was roaming about the place with braids swinging and torch swaying, crying:

"Good night, darlings! Good night all! Who goes home? What a *splendid* adventure we're all having!"

The rest of the Bagthorpe tribe pulled the bedclothes over their ears in varying degrees of disgust.

Only Mrs. Fosdyke, eyes wide open, lay sleepless through the silent watches of the night. Then, just before dawn, she finally dropped off into uneasy, nightmare-ridden slumber.

SIX

The Bagthorpes woke early next morning, partly because of the uncurtained windows, and partly because of a lot of noise, banging and yelling.

Mr. Bagthorpe had not had a much better night than Mrs. Fosdyke. He had the feeling that he was sharing the hut with other, unseen presences, though not necessarily of a supernatural order. Each time he heard various scufflings and scratchings he tried to catch these visitors unaware by suddenly directing on them the beam of his torch. He failed every time. He could not accept that this was possibly because his reflexes were slow.

Could it be, perhaps, a disembodied hand, clawing to get in? he wondered.

If this *were* the case, however, he thought that his fur (metaphorically speaking) should be standing up on end. He felt not even a prickling between the shoulder blades, not a hint of gooseflesh.

What if I'm one of those people who can't see ghosts, even when they're right in front of their noses? he thought moodily. I'll have wasted my time coming to this godforsaken place. And I'll have to scrap my script.

This morbid train of thought went on for most of the night. Everybody, it seemed, could cash in on the current vogue for ghost stories, except himself. There it was again—on with the torch—snap! Nothing. Off with the torch. Six weeks cooped up in purgatory with Grandma and Mrs. Fosdyke. The worst possibility he could envisage, the thought of which *did* bring him out in a cold sweat, was that Mrs. Fosdyke should turn out able to see the legion ghosts that Mr. Jones claimed stalked the house nightly, and not himself.

If that miserable hedgehog can see ghosts and I can't, he thought, I shall kill myself.

By dawn, then, Mr. Bagthorpe was in a state verging on paranoia. As the light strengthened, he saw with distaste the extent of the fungus, mold, dirt and insect life surrounding him.

There are more creepy crawlies within these four walls, he thought, than David Bellamy has seen in a lifetime. I may even drop him a line.

He was in an extremely bad temper even before he got back to *Ty Cilion Duon* and found himself locked out.

"Hell's *bells!*" he exclaimed, his teeth chattering in the dawn chill. "What if I had come down with appendicitis in the night? What if I had been attacked by a wild dog and contracted rabies?"

The house remained silent.

"Get up!" he yelled. "Let me in! Where *are* you, for crying out loud? What's the matter with you? You're emotional cripples, the lot of you! Wake up! Let me in!"

This little speech of familial affection and goodwill was interspersed with thundering blows on the door.

The day was off to a good start.

Mr. Bagthorpe's cup was full when the door was finally opened. He stood, teeth bared, face to face with Grandma.

"Good morning, Henry," she said. "I trust you had a restful night?"

He lurched past her wordlessly, clutching his stubble. He came to an abrupt halt as he saw, in full daylight, the true awfulness of his holiday accommodation. He stared wildly at the rusty boiler, the resident spiders and cockroaches, the cracked sink, the dusty floor.

"Oh my God!" he groaned. "And I thought *home* was hell!"

"You have made your bed, Henry," Grandma told him sanctimoniously, "and you must lie on it. Unfortunately, so must the rest of us, innocent parties to your crackpot scheme. This kitchen would certainly be of interest to any Inspector of Hygiene."

By now the rest of the Bagthorpes were emerging, bleary-eyed and ill-tempered at the rude manner of their awakening.

They soon discovered that they had eaten their intended breakfast the night before. Milkless cereals were distributed and eaten unsmilingly. Mrs. Fosdyke mercifully snored through this undistinguished meal. When Mr. Bagthorpe clumsily attempted to pin the blame for everything on her, he was again rounded upon by the rest (with the exception of Grandpa, who looked merely bewildered. There again, he usually did look bewildered, even at home. He probably was, most of the time.).

"Mrs. Fosdyke played no part whatever in this miserable debacle," Mrs. Bagthorpe told him. "It may even make her seriously ill. If this is the case, then it will be our duty to nurse her back to health."

"Duty?" echoed Mr. Bagthorpe. "Nurse—ashoo!"

"There, you see," said his wife coldly. "The moment you are confronted by an unpleasant truth, you commence sneezing."

"My—ashoo!—entire life is a-shoo!—unpleasant truth," he returned. "And rendered the—shoo!—more so by that interminable—shoo!—hedgehog. She clearly foresaw this whole—ashoo!—thing, and accompanied us only because she wished to report—shoo!—back to those crones in the snug at The Fiddler's Arms."

"Nobody who saw Mrs. Fosdyke's face last night," Mrs. Bagthorpe replied, "could possibly accuse her of foreseeing anything. She looked, Henry, like one looking into the mouth of hell. I will not have a word said against her."

Breakfast over, Mrs. Bagthorpe tried to draw up a Plan of Campaign.

"We must obviously stay here," she said, "until you, Henry, have contacted your Mr. Jones and obtained a refund. In the meantime, we must endeavor to make the place more habitable, and improve the quality of life. There are certain things we shall need from the Village Stores, and—"

Her offspring here all loudly volunteered for this errand. First, there was the prospect of buying extra rations, and secondly, the journey could be spun out as long as possible in order to avoid other, less pleasant, household duties. Unfortunately for them, Mrs. Bagthorpe said that she herself would make the trip.

"I shall take the car," she said. "We need all kinds of cleaning materials. Far too much for any of you to carry."

"I'll go with you," Mr. Bagthorpe said. "I have to make some phone calls."

His style was being considerably cramped by lack of a phone to shout into. Long lines were to form outside the Llosilly telephone box during the ensuing days.

"Where's all my stuff?" he demanded.

"It is still in the hall, Henry," his wife replied.

He went out and began to rummage in the still monumental heap of luggage. After a time he came back.

"Look, Laura," he said, "among my folders, in fact on top of them, and secured by an elastic band, was a long buff envelope. It contains the correspondence I had with that trickster Jones, including his address and phone number. Without it, we are lost."

"Have another look," she told him. She was not really listening, engaged as she was in making a very long list.

"You lot!" said Mr. Bagthorpe. "Have you been foraging in my things?"

"No, Father," they chorused.

He went out again. Jack had a sudden awful thought. Daisy and Billy Goat Gruff had been wandering about unsupervised while the luggage was being loaded. And Daisy seemed obsessed by the theory that the choicest morsels she could offer to her pet consisted of Mr. Bagthorpe's papers. Could it be that Mr. Jones's address had gone the same way as Mr. Bagthorpe's income tax rebate?

He wisely decided against voicing this theory, for fear of attracting his father's wrath, but to let him finally add two and two together for himself. When he did, his fury was extreme.

"We're finished," he said at last, having delivered a very long and unflattering speech about Daisy and her goat. "We shall have to stop here forever."

"Nonsense, dear," said his wife. "I think *I* made a note of the phone number when I made the call about the—the cottage."

"Hovel," he corrected her.

She fetched her diary and leafed through it. Her brow furrowed.

"Oh, dear," she said, "I seem to have three or four numbers here with no name attached to them. How very careless of me. However, I'm certain it's *one* of these."

She copied out four telephone numbers and passed them to him. He eyed them bitterly.

"I stand as much chance of tracking down Jones on one of these," he said, "as getting put straight through to the hot line for the Kremlin."

He and Mrs. Bagthorpe set off for the village, leaving the other members of the family to their various pursuits. Grandpa retreated to the sitting room to fiddle with his blizzard and Grandma to her room to Breathe. The younger Bagthorpes set about staking out their territories, with a good deal of noisy argument. They then, with the exception of Jack, set about practicing their musical instruments. The racket this made was execrable. The acoustics of the house, because of the lack of carpets and other soft furnishings, were considerably superior to those in the Albert Hall. The Bagthorpes rattled around in it, as Mr. Bagthorpe later said, like dried peas in a tin.

Mrs. Fosdyke stirred in her sleep, made little moaning noises, and finally awoke. Nobody would ever know how she felt during those first seconds when she surfaced to consciousness and remembered where she was. She would try to describe her feelings, time and again, to Mesdames Pye and Bates, but never came anywhere near giving a true picture. There weren't any words, she said, that *could* describe it.

Matters were not helped by the discordant strains of oboe, cello and drums. Mrs. Fosdyke had heard these before, of course, but at Unicorn House they were more muffled and far away, because of the presence of carpets and curtains. Also, the younger Bagthorpes used their musical instruments in much the same way as their father used the phone, and on the present occasion had plenty of ill temper to discharge.

Mrs. Fosdyke lay for quite a long time remembering the previous evening, and the state of her new kitchen, before actually going down and facing the reality.

Meanwhile, down in the village, Mr. Bagthorpe was in the process of alienating the local inhabitants. He had no gift at all for the social niceties, and in fact did not have a single friend in the world.

His first blunder was to make a facetious remark about the name Jones, which also happened to be the name of the postmaster from whom Mr. Bagthorpe had just demanded five pounds in silver, for use in the call box. When the postmaster coldly informed him of this fact, Mr. Bagthorpe made no attempt to salvage the situation.

"Ha! Jones the Post, eh?" he said. "Or is it Jones the Stamp? Or Jones the Sorry Wrong Number? Ha!"

This was to cost Mr. Bagthorpe dearly in his efforts to track down the particular scion of the Jones family who had rented him *Ty Cilion Duon.*

All he had was a selection of telephone numbers, none of which, he thought gloomily, looked very Welsh. When he had rung all these numbers and got no reply from any of them, he got on to the directory of inquiries. Here he succeeded in making more enemies, including the supervisor.

"*Why* cannot I be given his address?" he yelled. "What's the matter with you? Why am I paying taxes?"

After this, by way of light relief, he put a call through to

The Knoll, with the intention of informing Uncle Parker of Daisy's feeding important documents to her goat.

If we can't turn up Jones, he thought, I might be able to go after Russell for a full refund.

To his intense frustration he could get no reply. He let the telephone ring for a full five minutes before he finally gave up hope.

The goat, he thought, has probably chewed through the wire. With any luck, it'll have electrocuted itself and its accursed owner, and the pair of them'll be incinerated to a crisp.

He finally slammed down the phone and stomped into the Village Stores, where his wife was filling wire baskets with every known brand of cleaner and disinfectant. There were several other shoppers in there, all speaking Welsh. Mr. Bagthorpe, immediately jumping to the conclusion that they were talking about him, glowered at these innocent ladies with such ferocity that they did, indeed, start talking about him.

"Ye gods!" he exclaimed in disgust. "Can they not speak English?"

By the time he and his wife left for the house, he had insured that any sympathy and cooperation in the village would be very thin on the ground. Had he known it, one of the shoppers had been the sister of the very Mr. Jones he was trying to track down.

When Mr. and Mrs. Bagthorpe arrived back at *Ty Cilion Duon*, staggering under boxloads of cleaning materials, it was to find Mrs. Fosdyke just entering the kitchen, still in her night attire. She did not wear a dressing gown because she had had no heart to unpack the night before. (Also, of course, there were no wardrobes.)

She came shuffling aimlessly in her fur-edged slippers. Mr.

Bagthorpe stared with ill-disguised distaste at the spectacle she presented. Her nightdress was of bright yellow seersucker dotted with pink rosebuds, and its proportions were not so much those of a garment as of a tent. (Mrs. Fosdyke made all her own nightdresses. She said that ones from the shops were skimped, and often caught fire.)

She was still wearing the same shell-shocked look as the night before. Mrs. Bagthorpe instantly dropped her boxes and hurried toward her.

"Oh, good *morning*, Mrs. Fosdyke. I do hope you slept well? Isn't it a lovely day? Henry and I have just been to get a few things because the house, in particular the kitchen, does seem to be rather underequipped. . . ."

"No sink . . ." Mrs. Fosdyke started on the refrain that had been running nonstop through her head for most of the night. "No sink, no fridge, no stove, no working surfaces. No dishwasher, no mixer, no Hoover . . . ."

At this Mr. Bagthorpe brightened a little. Even if there *were* some old Hoover hidden away somewhere, there were no carpets to *be* vacuumed. This, he reflected with satisfaction, would so severely curtail her normal activities that she would probably have a nervous breakdown.

Mrs. Fosdyke had paused in her litany only to take breath. On she droned, in a dull, relentless monotone.

"There'll be no joy in anything. How can I go on? How can I do with no cooker, no fridge, no—"

"Oh, I agree!" cried Mrs. Bagthorpe. "We all do. We all sympathize with you entirely and will do everything in our power to help you!"

What she was really afraid of was that Mrs. Fosdyke would catch the next train out of Wales, and leave *herself* with no cooker, no fridge, no . . . etc. On the other hand, Mrs. Fosdyke was at present in no fit state to travel, especially by train and unaccompanied. Wales, Mrs. Bagthorpe thought, was probably full of branch lines. Mrs. Fosdyke, in her dazed condition, could easily get lost in the network, and travel round and round Wales in endless circles. While this might strike Mr. Bagthorpe as a fitting fate for her, it was no part of Mrs. Bagthorpe's own scheme. She made a mental note to tell her offspring to butter up Mrs. Fosdyke as never before.

"Let's all have a cup of tea!" she suggested gaily.

Mrs. Fosdyke dully turned her eyes to Jack's camping stove.

"I ain't touching that," she said. "Them things is dangerous. There's thousands of them blow up every year. I've seen it in the papers."

At least now Mrs. Fosdyke was beginning to sound more like her old self.

"I'll see to the tea," Mrs. Bagthorpe told her. "And then we must look into the whole question of more suitable cooking arrangements."

Mrs. Fosdyke's gaze now moved to the boiler. The look she gave it was equally glassy.

"*Them* blow up, as well," she observed fatalistically.

Mrs. Bagthorpe passed a hand over her brow. The horrible mingling of her children's attacks on their musical instruments was no aid to clear thinking.

"Oh, dear!" she said desperately.

In a momentary lull there came the sound of tires on gravel. They had a visitor.

"Jones!" exclaimed Mr. Bagthorpe grimly. "Right!"

Mrs. Bagthorpe shook her head. That particular sound of tires on gravel seemed to stir a memory.

How silly! she told herself. They are hundreds of miles away!

The three in the kitchen waited. They heard the long, reverberating creak as the front door swung slowly open. "Hullo, there!" came a familiar voice. "Anyone at home?" "Zack, Zack!" cried a voice equally familiar. "Zack, bring Zero quick! Billy Goat Gruff's come to play!"

Mr. Bagthorpe groaned.

SEVEN

The Bagthorpe annals had always had their moments of surprise, but this one was in a class of its own. Afterward, the whole family tried to pin down in words the exact degree of shock they had felt at the time.

"It was like finding a crocodile in your soup," said Rosie.

"Or opening a broom cupboard, and the mummified body of Queen Victoria toppling out on you," said William.

"Or getting a telegram to say you'd won the pools," Jack offered.

"Don't be silly," Tess told him. "To me, it was as if all the trees in the garden had burst out singing the Hallelujah Chorus."

The others looked askance at this.

"It is well known, in theory, that trees *can* sing," Tess told them. "I am simply quantifying the degree of shock one would experience were one to actually hear them."

"Do not go about this family promulgating *that* kind of half-baked notion," said Mr. Bagthorpe, who had little time for other people's half-baked theories. "Personally, when I heard the voices of Russell and that deranged daughter of his in the hall, the shock could not have been greater if a cobra had come out at me from a letter box. It is a good thing I have a strong heart, or I'd have been a goner."

At the time, Mr. Bagthorpe's face had become so suffused with purple that one or two of the family had thought it probable that he *was* having a heart attack.

Uncle Parker entered the kitchen. He looked outstandingly elegant, possibly more so than usual, in contrast to such outstandingly inelegant surroundings. At his heels came Daisy with the goat in tow.

"Zack, tell Zero to come and play," she squealed, without preliminaries.

Zero was not, in fact, very interested in the goat. He would walk over and sniff it, and then walk away again. Jack thought this very intelligent of him.

After all, dogs have got a sense of smell about a thousand times stronger than ours, he thought. And that goat certainly does stink. Zero could get overcome by it, or even poisoned.

"Isn't anyone going to say hello?" inquired Uncle Parker. "Aren't you surprised to see us?"

"Certainly we are, Russell," said Mrs. Bagthorpe weakly. "But where is dear Celia?"

"Celia's nerves are rather overstrained by the journey," he replied. "She is lying down and trying to catch the odd poetic thought."

"In the *car*?" asked Mrs. Bagthorpe, puzzled.

"What," choked Mr. Bagthorpe, "what, in the name of all that is wonderful, are you doing here? Who invited him? Who told him where we were?"

He glowered about him.

"I, Henry, naturally gave Daisy my temporary address," Grandma told him coolly. "So that we could exchange letters. Daisy is an outstanding correspondent, a born letter-writer."

This was true. Daisy and Grandma exchanged frequent letters, even at home. These missives kept the Bagthorpes in a constant state of nervous apprehension. If there were a sudden spate of them, they could be sure that The Unholy Alliance was hatching something up.

"An' we've come to Wales to see some dragons," piped up that tireless child. "An' I going to have a little dragon all of my own to play with Billy Goat Gruff!"

Uncle Parker was now looking about him with an air of amused superiority that was not wasted on Mr. Bagthorpe.

"By Jove, Henry," he said, "you look to be rather short on creature comforts. I should never have connected *you* with living rough."

"Then you would be mistaken," snapped Mr. Bagthorpe. "I am a great believer in living rough. It is character-building. I have brought my family here with the express intention of toughening them up."

The rest of the family gaped as he uttered this barefaced lie.

"It is something that you, Russell, wouldn't understand," he went on. "Your entire existence is little more than a non-stop cocktail party. You would not last five minutes in a Benedictine monastery. You are a slave to luxury."

"Well, yes, I am, rather," agreed Uncle Parker mildly. "I have to agree with you there, Henry."

He looked about the room again, his gaze lingering on the cracked sink, scattered camping equipment and monolithic boiler.

"Where did you *find* such a place?" he inquired. "Surely not through the Automobile Association? You must have had to turn every stone to find anything so character-building as this. It resembles, if I may say so, a Victorian dosshouse."

Mr. Bagthorpe looked apoplectic again. This was the last turn of the screw. He had thought himself in purgatory already. But that Uncle Parker should witness the awfulness and squalor of his holiday home was more than he could take. He was now in hell.

"Father took it because it's haunted," Jack told Uncle

Parker. He could not help feeling sorry for Mr. Bagthorpe, caught at such a towering disadvantage and without a single card in his hand. "We didn't see any ghosts last night, because we were too tired, but I expect we shall tonight."

"Oooh!" squealed Daisy. "Ghosties! Daddy, Daddy, *I* want a ghostie!"

"Get her one, Russell," Mr. Bagthorpe advised him. "With any luck, she'll then transfer her affections from that reeking goat."

"As a matter of fact," Uncle Parked drawled, "I rather think the pile we're stopping in *does* boast the odd Gray Lady or Faceless Monk."

This speech was followed by an unusually long silence. The Bagthorpes were practically never silent.

"Stopping?" croaked Mr. Bagthorpe at last. "Did you say— *stopping?*"

"We on our holidays," confided Daisy, "me and Mummy and Daddy and Billy Goat Gruff. And we stopping in a real live castle!"

"A castle?" exclaimed Grandma. "How very interesting, Daisy. Does it have hot and cold water, and a modern kitchen?"

"Oooh, it's lovely," Daisy told her. "It got suits of armor and dead tigers, and it got big beds up to the ceiling like Sleeping Beauty!"

"And I imagine that the food is delicious?" prompted Grandma, who certainly knew how to needle people.

"Well, I had soup and ducks and chips," Daisy nodded. "And the nice waiter man kep' fetching me ice cream in all different colors."

The Bagthorpes, remembering their milkless cereal, gazed at Daisy with pure hatred.

"The food *is* splendid," Uncle Parker agreed. "A very nice line in lobster thermidor, and first-rate vichyssoise. There again, it might not be up to *your* standards, Henry. You, after all, are blessed with Mrs. Fosdyke."

He bowed gallantly toward that lady, without betraying even a flicker of surprise at her marquee of a nightdress. He was very good at picking his words. He knew that Mr. Bagthorpe would never, ever, put Mrs. Fosdyke and "blessed" in the same sentence.

Mrs. Fosdyke appeared not to hear Uncle Parker's compliment. She had collapsed into a deckchair and was looking far away again. She wore rather the kind of expression, Jack thought, that he had himself aimed for in his Vision-seeing days.

"Come on!" urged Daisy impatiently. She, in common with the rest of the Bagthorpe tribe, had a very low boredom threshold. It was partly this that made her so dangerous. "Come on, Grandma, let's go and look for ghosties."

"Certainly, dear child," responded Grandma. "We will take up a saucer of milk for Thomas the Second. Where did you put the milk, Laura?"

"Not in the fridge," murmured Uncle Parker. "One might as well be up the Amazon."

"Oh, dear!" Mrs. Bagthorpe clapped a hand to her mouth, dismayed. "I quite forgot! One is so used to milk being delivered daily that one never thinks . . . and . . . and I was so taken up with purchasing cleaning materials."

"Part of the toughening up process, I take it, Henry," said

Uncle Parker. "Test of *anyone's* character, I should think, cleaning this lot up. My congratulations."

"I cannot feed disinfectant to the cat, Laura," Grandma told her coldly. "I do think that a helpless, innocent cat ought to be able to rely on a saucer of milk daily."

"Of course," agreed Mrs. Bagthorpe weakly. "Jack, dear, would you—?"

"I'll go!" chorused her offspring in unison.

"*I'll* go," said Mr. Bagthorpe. He had noticed a pub called The Welsh Harp opposite the post office.

A pub's one of the best places for making inquiries about missing persons, he thought. If I spend a bit of time in there, I might get a lead on Jones.

He made for the door and turned.

"And don't let *her* out of your sight," he ordered. "It's ten to one this place isn't even insured."

When he had gone, Mrs. Bagthorpe made an effort to be gracious and hostesslike.

"How lovely to see you, anyway, Russell," she told him, "and how nice that Celia and yourself are staying nearby."

"Just up the road," he told her. "In fact, I should think you could see the odd turret from here."

Up to this point none of the Bagthorpes had shown much interest in the scenery. Now they hurried to investigate. From Jack's and William's room they saw, sure enough, a splendid stone castle beyond the trees.

"That's it," Uncle Parker told them laconically. He glanced about the room, taking in the absence of curtains, carpets, wardrobes and drawers.

"I'm bound to say, Laura," he observed, "that one is forced to have a sneaking admiration for poor old Henry. He could not have found a place with fewer creature comforts than this."

Mrs. Bagthorpe bridled at this reference to her husband.

"He, of course, is a sensitive, creative writer," she told him coldly. (Normally, she denied this.) "His values are entirely different from those of the rest of us ordinary mortals."

Mr. Bagthorpe could not have expressed this better himself.

"Well, yes," agreed Uncle Parker, "I have often thought so myself. I mean, I cannot think of a single ordinary mortal I know who would stop twenty-four hours in this benighted hole, let alone six weeks. Good for Henry!"

"Where's the ghosties?" demanded Daisy. "And where's the dragons? There's *fousands* of dragons in Wales, Mummy said so."

"Of course there are, darling child," Grandma told her. "And we will search for them together. Come to my room, and we will arrange my photographs and treasures."

Off they went. The others stared bleakly after them. If the pair of them ran true to form, there was trouble in the offing.

"I think Daisy's a bad influence on Grandma," Jack said.

"You shut up, Jack Bagthorpe," said Rosie, who always stuck up for Daisy. "She's sweet."

"Like strychnine, she is," William said.

"Don't mind me," said Uncle Parker. "But try to moderate your language about Daisy in front of Celia, won't you?"

"Let's all go down," said Mrs. Bagthorpe. "Henry will be back in a moment with the milk, and then we will all have coffee."

Here she was wrong. Mr. Bagthorpe was not back in a moment, nor even in half an hour, and even when he did return, he had overlooked the milk. He was in The Welsh Harp, conscientiously pursuing his inquiries and making a whole lot more enemies in the process. In the end, Uncle Parker got tired of waiting for coffee, and left.

"I must get back to Celia," he said. "She is not used to castles, and may be picking up ancient, hostile vibrations."

"I want to stop with Grandma," piped up Daisy.

No one much liked the sound of this.

"You won't get much to eat," Jack told her.

"I full up. I had crispies and I had bacon and I had egg and I had sausages and millions of toast," Daisy told her unfortunate audience.

"Do they *let* her have that goat at the castle?" Tess asked. "Does it count as a dog, or what?"

"I know the fellow who owns it," said Uncle Parker. "No problem."

Jack could not help wondering what were the reactions of other guests when they suddenly encountered a goat in the lift or on the stairs. He also wondered where it made its puddles.

"I'll tell you what," said Uncle Parker, "I know you're all squatting in this hovel for the good of your souls, but why not come up to the castle and have a bite with us this evening?"

There was a clamor of acceptances of this invitation. Only Mrs. Bagthorpe and Mrs. Fosdyke made no response. The former was wearing her puckered brow, and the latter sat in her deckchair like a beached whale, apparently looking into eternity.

"It really is most kind, Russell," Mrs. Bagthorpe eventually said. "And I'm sure the children will be delighted, but—"

"And myself," put in Grandma. "It will make a welcome change to have an occasion to dress for, and to see silver service."

"But I don't really think I can speak for Henry," continued Mrs. Bagthorpe.

"Well, no," conceded Uncle Parker, "that would be somewhat rash. Poor old Henry."

He took a last look about him.

"Got to give him credit, though. He certainly knows how to suffer. Cheers, all!"

With that he was gone, leaving the Bagthorpes with Daisy and her goat. Seconds later, Mr. Bagthorpe arrived back, in a very bad temper. This was partly because he had drawn a blank in The Welsh Harp, and partly because he had narrowly missed a head-on collision with Uncle Parker in the drive.

"Hell's bells!" he gritted as he strode through the door and tripped over Rosie's easel.

"Ah, you're back, dear," his wife greeted him. "You have only just missed Russell."

"You can say that again," he told her. "By a centimeter, at a rough guess. Why must he pursue me even on my holidays?"

"He has invited us all up to the castle for a meal," she said. "Isn't that lovely?"

Here Mr. Bagthorpe found himself in a dilemma. He did not want to have salt rubbed in his wounds by being forced to witness the splendors of the Parkers' surroundings (with which his own would be in stark contrast). On the other hand, he enjoyed having rows with Uncle Parker, and was certainly ready for a good meal. He decided that he would accept the invitation, but only after making a great show of reluctance.

"I do not think we need his charity, Laura," he said.

"Oh, but it's not *that*," she protested. "I think it's partly to thank us for having Daisy, and partly . . . ." her voice trailed off.

"Did I hear you aright?" he said. "Are you mad, Laura?"

"But—but she's doing no harm," Mrs. Bagthorpe said. "She's only looking for dragons and ghosties—I mean ghosts."

Mr. Bagthorpe shook his head wearily for a very long time.

"Am I dreaming things," came a dull, flat voice, "or did I see that Daisy Parker just now?"

It was Mrs. Fosdyke, whom they had quite forgotten. They both turned. She was looking not at themselves, but straight ahead.

"Couldn't've been 'er, o' course," she went on. "Just a 'orrible nightmare. Shall I wake up? Shall I ever wake up?"

Mr. Bagthorpe let out a snort of disgust but his wife frowned warningly.

"Come along, Mrs. Fosdyke, dear," she said, going to her. "Let's go back upstairs and get dressed, shall we? Then I'll make a nice cup of coffee."

Mrs. Fosdyke allowed herself to be helped up and led away.

"Tea." she murmured as she went. "Tea . . . ."

"Of course," promised Mrs. Bagthorpe. "Tea."

Mrs. Fosdyke did not believe in coffee. She said it kept people awake all night and brought them out in spots. Also, it was foreign. Mrs. Bagthorpe had once tried to point out to her that so, too, was tea, but Mrs. Fosdyke would have none of it.

"Tea's our national drink," she said stubbornly. "Always has been."

"I suppose she thinks the whole of the Home Counties is one vast tea plantation," Mr. Bagthorpe had said later when he was told of this.

When Mrs. Bagthorpe had deposited Mrs. Fosdyke in her room, she returned to the kitchen followed by her children, whom she had rounded up. Daisy and the goat were holed up with Grandma and Thomas the Second. Grandpa was still in the sitting room studying his snowstorm.

"I am extremely worried about Mrs. Fosdyke," Mrs. Bagthorpe began.

"I have *always* been worried by Mrs. Fosdyke," said her husband. "Ha!"

"This is not a laughing matter," she told him quenchingly. "We must do one of two things. We must either get her to a doctor, or ourselves attempt to bring her out of shock."

"How?" demanded William.

"Well, I seem to remember reading or hearing about this theory . . . ," she said.

All the Bagthorpes had theories, from time to time. At any given moment, Unicorn House was swarming with theories. Rarely, however, were they held by Mrs. Bagthorpe, who was marginally more balanced than the others.

"What it said," she went on, "was that shock could be cured by another, greater shock."

There was a small silence as her listeners digested this notion.

"Like what?" Mr. Bagthorpe asked at last. "Putting a scorpion in her slipper?"

"But Fozzy's *used* to shocks," Jack objected. "She's *always* getting them."

This was unarguable.

"Then we must have a little competition," said Mrs. Bagthorpe. "See which one of us can think of the most original shock. And there will, of course, be a prize."

This threw a different light on things.

"And if anyone can think of a shock that'll finish her off, I'll donate an extra prize," said Mr. Bagthorpe. "Ha!"

EIGHT

Most of the family was now taken up by a power struggle, first to establish territories, and secondly to avoid as many chores as possible. Mr. Bagthorpe selected what was probably meant as the dining room for use as his study.

"And you lot keep out," he warned the rest of them. "And kindly refrain from banging about overhead."

He later discovered a hatch into the kitchen, which he could open and shout through.

Given that he was not prepared to spend another night with the unseen presences in the cottage, alternative sleeping arrangements had to be made.

"Me and Zero'll camp in the garden," Jack offered. "At least, we will when we've seen some of the ghosts."

"What exactly *are* these ghosts?" William asked. "What are we meant to be looking out for?"

"Originally, of course, I had a list of them," replied Mr. Bagthorpe, "before they were fed to that devilish goat. So far as I can remember, there is a Veiled Lady, a Small Child Weeping, a Bearded Man Carrying a Candle, a Disembodied Skull, a Ring of Blue Fire, emitting a high-pitched wail, and an Old Man Limping."

Silence.

"Crikey, Father," said Rosie at last, "you never swallowed all that lot?"

"What d'you mean?" he demanded.

"Well, I mean, nowhere's got that many ghosts. Even Borley Rectory hasn't got that many!"

"Rubbish," he told her tersely. "They have been accumulating over the centuries."

"But, Henry," said Mrs. Bagthorpe, "I would not put this house any earlier than mid-Victorian."

"That has nothing to do with it," he blustered.

"Father's right," put in Tess. "It could be an ancient site. It could lie on black ley lines."

No one had the foggiest idea what she was talking about, not even Mr. Bagthorpe, despite his recent research into hauntings.

"Absolutely," he said. "I was about to point that out myself."

Grandma now put her oar in.

"It seems to me, Henry," she said, "that if your elusive Mr. Jones was capable of renting this place as fit for human habitation, then he is a fantasist of the first water. He must have hugely enjoyed creating such an inventory of ghosts to take in a person so gullible as yourself."

"Bilge, Mother," Mr. Bagthorpe told her. Exactly the same thought had occurred to himself, as he sat moodily downing his beer amid the mute and unsmiling locals in The Welsh Harp.

"The proof of the pudding is in the eating," she told him. "When we have all seen this long list of ghosts, then we shall believe in them."

"There is no way you will ever see them," he returned. "You are not sufficiently highly tuned. Your vibrations are all to pot."

A first-class row seemed to be developing, and Mrs. Bagthorpe tried hastily to avert it.

"Jack, dear, you and William can have your sleeping bags in the sitting room," she said, "and then Mrs. Fosdyke can have your room."

"But Grandpa has the telly on till closedown," objected William.

"There is a limit, I should have thought," said Grandma, "to how long anyone can maintain interest in watching a snowstorm."

"P'raps he sees more in it than we do," said Jack, who was fond of Grandpa.

"Talking of which," said William, "I hope you all realize that I am now totally cut off from Anonymous from Grimsby."

"Just as your grandfather is cut off from 'Playschool,' " Mr. Bagthorpe told him.

"I expect it's the mountains," said Mrs. Bagthorpe wisely.

"Of *course* it's the mountains, Mother," said William. "But it's pretty galling to know that Anonymous from Grimsby is in constant touch with an Alien Intelligence from Outer Space, but can't even raise a bleep from mid-Wales."

"If I have told you once," said Mr. Bagthorpe, "I have told you a thousand times. If this fellow from Grimsby is receiving information from an Alien Intelligence, let him pass it on to the government. Let Whitehall deal with it."

"You don't understand," said William bitterly. "Nobody understands."

This was, by and large, true. Each individual Bagthorpe followed his own Strings to his Bow with relentless and single-minded passion. But there was very little overlapping. Nobody took the remotest interest in anyone else's Strings except now and then when jealousy crept in. On this occasion, William's desolation at being deprived for six whole weeks of a well-loved, if invisible, friend, left everyone else cold. All it did was remind others of what they, too, were missing.

"I shouldn't think there's a swimming pool within a hundred miles," complained Rosie. (Here she was to be proved wrong. Uncle Parker's castle boasted one with marble pillars and warm, turquoise water.)

"And I don't suppose there's anyone with whom I can conduct a conversation in advanced French," added Tess.

"Try the village," Mr. Bagthorpe advised. "They certainly talk *some* kind of quaint lingo—ha!"

"Fortunately," said Grandma, "I have my Breathing. That transcends all boundaries. It is multilingual."

"I have made a list," Mrs. Bagthorpe now revealed, "of activities we might all pursue while we are in Wales. Extra Strings to our Bows."

The Bagthorpes were all the time looking for fresh pursuits in which to channel their considerable energies, but on this occasion thought that she had got her priorities wrong.

"I don't feel strong enough to do anything," Rosie said. "My tummy really aches. I think it's hunger pangs. I can't even paint when I'm hungry."

"I think my blood sugar level is dangerously low," William said. "Certainly too low to do anything physical, like playing drums or tennis. Even if there was a court. There's nowhere flat enough around here to have a court."

"So how *are* we ever going to get anything decent to eat?" Tess asked. "Fozzy's obviously in a galloping decline. And even if she weren't, she's got no proper stove."

"I have been thinking of that," Mrs. Bagthorpe told them. "I think we must definitely supplement the present cooking facilities. I have thought of something that will fill the bill admirably, and at the same time be tremendous fun."

"What?" asked Rosie suspiciously. Mrs. Bagthorpe's idea of fun did not always, or even often, coincide with that of her offspring.

"We shall purchase a barbecue," she replied.

A small silence ensued while everyone considered this.

"I bet Fozzy doesn't like barbecues," said William. "At home, we've only ever had them in the evenings, after she's gone home."

"She definitely thinks they're foreign," Jack said. "She told me so."

This was ominous. Mrs. Fosdyke was no admirer of things foreign. Indeed, if she had obeyed her own deepest promptings, she would not now be sitting poleaxed in the middle of Wales.

"You certainly can't do steak and kidney pies on a barbecue," William pointed out. "Or meringues. Or pork pies. Or Yorkshire puddings. Or soufflés. Or—"

"*Don't* go on, dear," begged his mother. "I know all this. But once Mrs. Fosdyke is feeling better, she may be tempted to embrace a new approach."

Mrs. Fosdyke had never in the past been tempted to embrace any new approach, and in her current state, the likelihood of her doing so now seemed remote.

"The day that woman embraces a new approach," said Mr. Bagthorpe, voicing the thoughts of all present, "will be the day it rains mint sauce."

"Oh, Henry!" remonstrated his wife. "You are such a pessimist!"

"In this household," he returned, "it would be unwise to be anything else."

"I've just thought of something," Jack said.

The others looked at him, but without much enthusiasm. Jack's ideas were not rated very highly by his family. "About giving Fozzy a shock," he explained. "You know— to cure her. What if Tess was to run at her, and grab her in a Judo hold, and throw her over her shoulder?" They all sat picturing this. The very idea of Mrs. Fosdyke describing an arc in the air and landing in a heap over Tess's left shoulder was mind-boggling. Rosie collapsed in helpless giggles.

"As a matter of fact," said William, "that's not at all a bad idea."

"Thanks," said Jack humbly.

"But what if she breaks a leg," cried Mrs. Bagthorpe anxiously, "or even her neck?"

"Then we shall count our blessings and learn to live without her," said her husband, who could hardly wait to do this. "What an optimist you are, Laura."

"You, Henry, are a hypocrite, a whited sepulcher," Grandma told him. "You enjoy Mrs. Fosdyke's cookery at least as much as any one of us, and frequently take second helpings when you think that her back is turned."

"I'll think about that Judo throw," Tess told them. "But it's not easy for me to visualize throwing Fozzy. I think her face would put me off. I'd have to psych myself up to it."

"When can you do it?" William asked. "Do it fast, Tess. The longer you think about it, the worse it'll get. Like going to the dentist."

"After lunch, then," she said.

"What lunch?" demanded Rosie hopefully.

This was a good question. Mrs. Fosdyke was up in her room contemplating eternity, and even if she were not, she had already declined to use the cooking facilities at present available.

"We are going up to the castle for a splendid meal tonight," said Mrs. Bagthorpe. "Could we not manage with fresh fruit, and cheese?"

"No," replied her offspring as one.

All this time the Bagthorpes had failed to notice that Daisy was missing. *Her* blood sugar level was not made low by hunger, and she was in fine fettle, as busy and creative as usual. She wisely decided that it was best to wait till dark before making a serious attempt to corner a ghostie.

Eager as always to explore new horizons, she trotted about the house looking for an interest. She was temporarily halted by the sight of Tess's oboe. This she was never allowed near under normal circumstances. All the Bagthorpes had guarded their instruments very closely since the occasion when Daisy had tackled one of William's drums with a knife and fork, thus rendering it a total write-off. Spotting an unwatched oboe was, then, a bonus for Daisy.

She tried for some time to raise a note from it. The results were disappointing.

"P'raps I 'a'n't got enough puff," she told the goat. "*You* got a lot of puff. *You* do it."

The goat made no sign of its willingness or otherwise to participate in this experiment, and Daisy accordingly pushed the oboe into its mouth. Billy Goat Gruff sucked for a moment and then, obviously thinking the oboe stem lacking in flavor, brought his teeth smartly together and snapped off a good two inches. He chewed ruminatively for a few seconds, then spat it out.

"That *is* rude manners, Billy Goat Gruff," Daisy told her charge reprovingly.

She dropped the mutilated oboe and descended to the hall

where there was still a considerable pile of unsorted luggage. Rosie's easel she had already broken or set fire to so many times that it held no further interest. Paints, however, were perennially attractive. Daisy released the goat's ribbon while she daubed one or two quick slogans on the walls. The goat meanwhile placidly munched at the odd wire that trailed from the heap.

Daisy soon lost interest in her slogans. With her, interest in anything soon wore off. Mr. Bagthorpe would often say that by the time she was seven, the world would hold no further charm for her.

"She'll have done everything," he maintained, "tried it, and found it wanting. She will then, with any luck, go into a terminal attack of boredom."

Daisy raked the heap with a practiced eye.

"Now what . . . now what . . . ?" she muttered. "Oooh—a dragon!"

She fished out a large black bottle-shaped container with a satisfying picture of a red, fire-eating dragon emblazoned on its side.

"Oooh!" she told her inattentive goat. "It's dragon food! It's for breathing their fires!"

She could hardly believe her luck. All she had to do, she thought, was to scatter this food, and dragons would come flocking in droves, like pigeons to corn. They might even eat out of her hand. She was disappointed, when she finally managed to unscrew the cap, to find that the dragon food was liquid, and had a funny smell. She was not, however, deterred. (Daisy was, in fact, virtually undeterrable.)

"It's Dragon Water," she decided. "I'll sprinkle it, and then all the dragons'll come and lick it up and have a lovely picnic and make lots 'n' lots of flames!"

With Daisy, to think was to act. Off she skipped into the garden, clean forgetting Billy Goat Gruff. She left in her wake a little spattered trail of the Dragon Water.

Meanwhile, in the kitchen, policy was still being argued. William and Jack were to sleep in the sitting room until they had seen their quota of phantoms, and thereafter would camp in the garden. A barbecue was to be purchased, and large quantities of rump steak.

"Mrs. Fosdyke will eventually herself feel hungry," Mrs. Bagthorpe told the others, though without conviction, "and steak will be something delicious yet easy to tackle on the barbecue."

"Get decent steak," Mr. Bagthorpe advised. "Get it so's we can eat it raw, if it comes to the crunch."

"And you, Jack," Mrs. Bagthorpe went on, ignoring him, "can cook lunch on your camping stove. We have an ample supply of baked beans, I believe, and some tinned corned beef."

"The stove's nearly run out," Jack said. "I'll fetch some more meths." The methyl alcohol for the stove had been left with the luggage in the hall.

He went out into the hall and stopped dead. The goat, chewing steadily on a length of flex, regarded him with clear yellow eyes.

Good grief! Jack thought, that's off Father's tape recorder that he speaks his Great Thoughts into. Or else it's Tess's, that she was going to record the ghosts with.

It was, it later emerged, both.

Jack sniffed. His eye fell on a couple of tubes of oil, half squeezed, and still oozing on to what looked like Mrs. Fosdyke's umbrella. (One of Mrs. Fosdyke's wiser dicta was that it was always raining in Wales.) His gaze moved to the walls.

These were, in a sense, the best furnished aspect of *Ty Cilion Duon*, in that they were panelled, in mahogany.

ARRY AWK AND BILLY AND DRAGON AND GOSTIE IS MY BES FRENDS, he read. This sounded serious. Underneath it was scrawled:

GRAMMA BAG IS SILY AND DONT BELEEV IN GOSTIES.

This, on the other hand, sounded more promising. It looked like the beginnings of a rift in The Unholy Alliance, which could be only good news to everyone else.

This was not, unfortunately, the case. Later, Grandma got out of an earlier, unguarded statement, by saying that what she had meant was that she didn't believe in *cruelty* to ghosties.

"They are my favorite species, after cats," she declared, "and are very sensitive and easily frightened. I do not wish to hear of any person in this household persecuting or ill-treating them."

Jack stared hopelessly at Daisy's latest graffiti. He was not, however, sufficiently dazed to be unaware of yet another strong smell, besides those of oil paint and goat. He wheeled slowly to face the heap. His eyes went to Daisy's recent trail of Dragon Water.

She's got the meths, he thought.

NINE

When the news broke that Daisy had disappeared with the meths and, for all anyone knew, a box of matches, reactions within the family were in marked contrast. Mrs. Bagthorpe immediately hurried to the sitting room to tell Grandpa, now apparently mesmerized by his blizzard, to put out his pipe.

No one else was half so sensible.

The younger Bagthorpes were mainly concerned about the prospect of a cold meal. Mr. Bagthorpe said that if Daisy blew herself up, along with the goat, then the meal would be well lost.

"*Any* meal would be well lost," he said. "Any *number* of meals."

Grandma did not, as might have been expected of someone so devoted to Daisy, appear much concerned. She knew Daisy and the workings of her mind well enough to be aware that it was not *she* who was in danger, but everyone else in her vicinity. This did not prevent Grandma from adding to the general angst.

"It is to be hoped there are no hidden wells or pools out there," she remarked. "Has anyone yet surveyed the grounds? *Are* there any wells? Wales, I have heard, is full of wells. I should not like to think of darling Daisy and her goat down a well."

"Hell's bells, Mother, stop harping on wells," snapped Mr. Bagthorpe.

"The goat's still there," Jack said.

"Out! Out!" cried Mrs. Bagthorpe, re-entering the kitchen. "Everyone go and search for Daisy!"

Reluctantly the Bagthorpes scattered on this all too familiar mission, with the exception of Mr. Bagthorpe.

"I am going to my study," he said, "though I don't hold out any hopes of achieving any dialogue. For my next holiday, I may book in to the Tower of Babel, for some comparative peace and quiet."

By the time Mr. Bagthorpe discovered that the microphone of his recorder was inside the goat, the rest were too far afield to hear his yell of rage and despair.

This yell, unlike most that he uttered, was perfectly genuine. He had in fact, against all likelihood, *had* a Great Thought during the morning, and urgently wished to record it before it vanished forever.

"You brute!" Mr. Bagthorpe told the goat. "You evil, stinking, sacrilegious brute!"

The goat returned his gaze with calm yellow eyes. This look, quite mild and unconcerned, inflamed Mr. Bagthorpe further. He forgot about his early encounter with the animal, during which he himself had virtually had to scramble up a tree to escape its horns. He seized Mrs. Fosdyke's umbrella, and charged it.

There were no spectators of the epic battle and chase that followed. The goat, of course, could not speak, and so it was Mr. Bagthorpe's own version of it that went down in history. Its accuracy would certainly not have landed him a post as war correspondent for the *Times*.

"I lammed it, I beat it, I bashed it!" he said. "It was in its killing mood—I saw that by its eyes, a bright, livid red. The red of sheer blood-lust. It kept putting its head down and coming, and all I had was Fozzy's umbrella. It was a battle to the death, I knew that!"

What in fact happened was that at first, he and the goat executed a series of little dancing and sparring movements, rather as at the opening of a boxing round. This gradually increased in momentum, and as Mr. Bagthorpe and the goat were confronting one another across the heap of belongings, a good deal of stuff was trampled and stamped upon. (This, in turn, led inevitably to yet another protracted series of rows with Uncle Parker about insurance liability.) In the end, Mr. Bagthorpe did manage to fetch Billy Goat Gruff a couple of fairly smart thwacks with the umbrella.

The goat's dander was then well and truly up. It put its head down and charged. Mr. Bagthorpe yelped, and dodged sideways in unconscious imitation of a matador in a bullfight he had once watched.

The spectacle that then followed was one that would have been deeply humiliating to Mr. Bagthorpe had it been witnessed, or recorded on film. It consisted mainly of Mr. Bagthorpe running. Hither and thither he ran, making fruitless sweeps with the umbrella, and showing a nimbleness of footwork that would have done credit to an international center forward. At one stage he ran into the sitting room, but was not fast enough to slam the door behind him. The goat charged on straight past him and put a hoof right into Grandpa's snowstorm.

By the time Billy Goat Gruff had extricated himself and turned around, Mr. Bagthorpe was already nearly halfway up the stairs.

Meanwhile Mrs. Fosdyke, still sitting numbly on the bed

and dismally rehearsing her list of missing kitchen equipment, became ever so vaguely aware of the commotion raging below. She was, of course, virtually immune to rows, after so many years with the Bagthorpes. Her decibel tolerance was probably as high as anyone's in the world.

This racket, however, was of such an order that it penetrated even her present foggy consciousness. She rose from the bed and went slowly out and onto the landing.

It was here that Mr. Bagthorpe ran into her, full tilt. Although far from being an athlete, he was running so fast that his momentum carried them both a fair distance. He yelped, dropped the umbrella, clutched at Mrs. Fosdyke, and the pair of them whirled on down the landing for all the world as if they were dancing a particularly spirited Gay Gordons.

The goat came on after them, head down. Mr. Bagthorpe had enough presence of mind to bring the dance to a stop with Mrs. Fosdyke between himself and his adversary, a human shield. The goat charged. Mrs. Fosdyke shrieked.

It was the marquee of a nightdress that saved her. The goat went for a part of it that was still swinging out to one side, as a result of her momentum. There was a loud ripping sound, followed by a dull thud as the goat rammed its head against the wall beyond, and next minute Mr. Bagthorpe and his partner were safe inside the bedroom, the door banged shut.

He leaned against the door, breathing heavily and listening for sounds of activity on the other side. He became aware of a sticky feeling on his right hand. He held it up, saw a bright scarlet gash, and slid gently into a heap to the floor.

When Mr. Bagthorpe came to, it was to feel cold water dripping onto his face. He opened his eyes. There, above him, only inches away, it seemed, was the face of Mrs. Fosdyke.

He hastily shut his eyes again and lay there, with a clothful of cold water still being squeezed over him.

Where am I? he wondered. Am I dead, and in hell?

This seemed a likely explanation.

That goat finally killed me, he told himself. I told them it was a killer, but they wouldn't believe me. They'll be sorry now. Serve 'em right.

He lay contemplating this thought with satisfaction. Gradually, however, he began to see odd snatches of recent events floating before him, in a kind of fractured action replay. He mentally reconstructed his Gay Gordons with Mrs. Fosdyke, the goat's charge, his own slamming of the door.

I *can't* be dead, he concluded.

He decided to risk opening his eyes again. He was fed up with having cold water dripped on him.

"It'd be better if 'e could get 'is head down between his knees," he heard Mrs. Fosdyke telling herself. "It's taking 'im long enough to come round. I don't know, I really don't! A grown man, frightened to death of a dumb animal. Great namby-pamby, him!"

At this slander, Mr. Bagthorpe *did* rouse himself. He did this so definitively, suddenly coming up to a sitting position, that he narrowly missed banging heads with Mrs. Fosdyke. She let out a squeak of surprise and dropped her cloth.

"Where am I?" he asked, in the best tradition. "What has happened?"

"You fainted!" she told him scornfully. "Went right off—frightened to death of that goat!"

"I most certainly was not, I—" he broke off, staring again in horror at his gashed right hand. He shut his eyes quickly, feeling himself in danger of going off again.

Mr. Bagthorpe could not stand the sight of blood. He defended this apparent weakness by saying that all the best people had it in common.

"Mahatma Gandhi could not bear the sight of blood," he would maintain. "Nor John Keats. It was partly that that killed him. Nor Florence Nightingale."

Grandma would sometimes argue about this latter instance, when she felt like it, and ask him how, in that case, Florence Nightingale had survived the Crimean War.

"By delegating," he told her. "She was Top Nurse, and got the others to do the dressings. All she did was go round swinging her lamp. Look it up. It's a historical fact."

On this occasion it would be hideously embarrassing for Mr. Bagthorpe when what he had taken to be a severe injury to his Writing Hand turned out to be red oil paint. This had transferred itself from Mrs. Fosdyke's umbrella during his fight with the goat. As yet, however, he still believed himself wounded.

"What you got your eyes shut for again?" he heard Mrs. Fosdyke demand. She sounded very unlike a ministering angel. "Open 'em, and stand up! What's all that red stuff you've got on you?"

Here Mr. Bagthorpe winced. He knew that Mrs. Fosdyke had once gone to evening classes given by the St. John's Ambulance Brigade. This had turned her almost overnight into an authority on most injuries that flesh is heir to. She was very dogmatic on the subject of splints and slings, bandages and tourniquets. On no account did he want her attempting to treat his injured Writing Hand.

If it has to be amputated as a result, we're all finished, he thought.

"It's *paint*!" he heard Mrs. Fosdyke's disgusted voice exclaim. " 'E's got paint all over 'im. I don't know, I really don't.

Is 'e going to open 'is eyes, or isn't he? And where's everybody else? I can't be standing over '*im* all day, I've got better things to do!"

With this she evidently replenished her cloth from her bowl of cold water, and squeezed it violently over Mr. Bagthorpe's already dripping head. This had the desired effect. He shot to his feet in a single movement.

"What the blazes do you think you're doing?" he yelled. "Are you mad? Where *is* everybody?"

He strode to the door, intending to slam out, remembered the goat, and stopped dead. He put his ear to the door and listened.

"*Now* what?" he heard Mrs. Fosdyke say behind him. " 'E's definitely unhinged, 'e really is."

Mr. Bagthorpe could hear what sounded like the return of the search party down below. Cautiously he inched open the door and peered through the crack. There was no sign of the goat. He remembered the dull thud as his adversary had charged through Mrs. Fosdyke's nightdress and into the wall.

Could've killed it, he thought. Concussed it, at any rate.

Reassured, he stepped nervously onto the landing. The goat was not lying in a heap against the wall, as he had hoped, but nor was it anywhere in sight. Downstairs, a moderate furor seemed to be building up. Mr. Bagthorpe, not wishing to miss this, slowly made his way down. He took care not to look at his hand, or his red-spattered clothing.

"Even now I *know* it's paint, it could still make me pass out," he told himself. "I'm so sensitive and imaginative that I could easily see it intuitively as blood."

Judging by the racket going on in the hall, there could now be blood being spilled all over everywhere. In his confused state it was at first difficult for him to disentangle the various strands of the argument.

People were diving into the entangled mass of property that had been trampled upon by Mr. Bagthorpe and the goat, and wildly waving their damaged belongings at one another. Tess was screaming about her lost microphone (she had yet to discover her abbreviated oboe) and gabbling incoherently about pyramids. William was brandishing in either hand two tennis rackets, both with hopeless-looking holes in the strings and gut trailing everywhere. Mrs. Bagthorpe was helplessly lifting out various expensive articles liberally smeared with different-colored oil paints. Of Grandma and Daisy there was no sign.

Mr. Bagthorpe had to think fast. He was in a dilemma. He wanted everybody to know about Daisy's goat trying to kill him again. On the other hand, he did not want to be identified as one who had broken half the stuff that was now being waved about.

I'll say the goat did it all, he decided. I'll say I found it destroying everything, and went after it.

This he proceeded to do. He gave an almighty shout, loud enough to be heard above the existing din, and made a dramatic descent. He commanded attention mainly because from a distance he really did look bloodstained, and as if his Writing Hand had been mangled.

He then went on to give his own version of what had transpired between the goat and himself. He left out, naturally, the bit about using Mrs. Fosdyke as a human shield, and said instead that he had rescued her. (This was the thinnest part of his story. The likelihood of it struck most of his audience as being nil.) He also left out the fainting.

"And to crown all," he finished, "the brute has obliterated Father's television. Put his damn great hoof straight through it."

"Where is the creature now?" his wife inquired.

"I have no idea," he replied. "I suppose I should have finished it off, while I had the chance. But I have, as you know, a soft spot where animals are concerned."

"Oooh, what a fib!" shrieked Rosie, speaking for them all. "Where is the poor little goat? And what about poor little Daisy? This time, I *shall* report you to the R.S.P.C.A.!"

She looked hopefully about for support from her family, but concern for poor little Daisy was at a very low ebb.

"Poor little Daisy," William told her, "has been sprinkling methyl alcohol all over the place like there was no tomorrow. Which there probably won't be," he added, "if anyone strikes a match."

"Also," supplied Tess bitterly, "Jack's camping stove is now nonoperational. It will be cold beans for lunch. I think this whole thing may give me anorexia nervosa."

Nobody cared about this, either. The Bagthorpes, with the exception of Jack, were not strong on empathy with the plight of others. They were all pure ego, rock hard.

They stood there, silent and bitter, among their ruined possessions. Their six weeks' holiday stretched before them like a spell in Sing Sing.

Mrs. Fosdyke had never, to date, shown any signs of having a sense of timing. Now, appearing at the head of the stairs, she could have left Sybil Thorndyke standing in this department.

"Would you *believe!*" she exclaimed, in familiar tones—a blend of disgust and disbelief.

The Bagthorpes, stunned, raised their eyes to where she

stood on the top stair. They took in the swathed turban that usually heralded a spring clean, the wrapround pinafore, the fur-edged slippers.

They watched numbly as she began her descent.

"They talk about home from home," they heard her say to herself. "Oh, yes, heard that dozens of times, I have. Never knew what they was talking about, neither. Wasn't like nome from home when I went for a week to that guesthouse in Great Yarmouth. *Nor* when I went to Bognor. But if *this* ain't home from home, then I don't know what is. You wouldn't think folks'd 'ave to go hundreds and hundreds of miles, just to land up . . . ."

On and on she went. The Bagthorpes, awestruck, exchanged looks of wonder.

Mrs. Fosdyke was herself again.

TEN

It was, of course, the shock of being charged by the goat (and possibly that of finding herself clasped in Mr. Bagthorpe's arms) that had restored Mrs. Fosdyke. She was immune to most shocks, but had never till now been charged by a goat. (Nor had she ever harbored romantic fantasies about herself and her employer.)

The swing in her mood was dramatic. From a state of hopeless apathy she went into top gear, feverishly scrubbing, banging, scooting and grumbling.

"She must be manic-depressive," Tess said, "with extra-violent mood swings. Even more than you, Father."

Mr. Bagthorpe did not care to be bracketed with Mrs. Fosdyke, let alone have her classed as a more interesting psychiatric case than himself. He had rather enjoyed his own condition ever since reading that Shakespeare had in all probability been a fellow manic-depressive.

"As, indeed, all great creative artists are," he would tell the family.

Mrs. Fosdyke's cooking was certainly of a high order, but by no stretch of the imagination, he felt, could she be described as a great creative artist. He found it particularly galling that it was he himself who had been unwittingly responsible for her present manic state, and that people kept congratulating him on this. Tess was especially warm in her praise.

"Jolly good, Father," she told him. "If the goat hadn't

charged her, *I* should've had to. I don't think I could ever have psyched myself up to do it. I can't seem to think of her as a human being."

"Amen to that," he replied. "All get going and make a list of your broken stuff. I'll take the bill up to Russell tonight."

"But that hardly seems gracious, Henry," Mrs. Bagthorpe protested. "We are, after all, going up to the castle as his guests."

"Graciousness has nothing to do with it," he told her. "And how much graciousness have we ever had out of that deranged daughter of his? Where's she now? What's she doing?"

Daisy and Grandma were still out in the grounds somewhere, looking for dragons. The search party had eventually discovered Daisy seated in some overgrown shrubbery, waiting for a dragon to take her bait, which had been liberally sprinkled in a clearing. Far from being grateful, Daisy had squealed furiously at her rescuers:

"Go 'way! Go 'way! You'll frighten all the little dragons!"

This was probably true. If there *were* any dragons, they in all likelihood *would* be frightened of the Bagthorpes.

"Go!" Grandma commanded the rest. "You should be ashamed of yourselves, interfering with the simple pleasures of an innocent child."

Back at the house, once they had witnessed Mrs. Fosdyke's return to all-out normality, the family engaged themselves in keeping out of her way. They rapidly downed their cold beans and corned beef, and scattered. Mr. Bagthorpe, accompanied by Tess and William, drove off to the nearest town in search of spare parts, such as microphones, flex, racket strings, oboe mouthpieces, flash equipment and so forth. He also had orders to purchase a barbecue and steak. Grandpa, strangely enough showing no sign of bereavement over his lost snowstorm, collected what was left of his fishing tackle and went off in search of a pool or stream. Rosie holed herself up in her room, announcing that she intended to paint a portrait of a dragon, as a gift for Daisy.

"And to make up for you all being so horrible to her," she told the others.

The house, then, fell strangely quiet. Jack, whittling at a model glider that had mercifully escaped the attention of the goat, was made uneasy by this unaccustomed peace. In the distance he could hear muffled sounds, made by his mother and Mrs. Fosdyke in their concerted attack on the kitchen. But the hush in the large, almost empty room where he sat seemed total.

"I wouldn't be surprised, old chap, if this house *was* haunted," he told Zero. "It feels pretty creepy to me, and it's broad daylight. So what must it be like at the stroke of midnight?"

Zero moved his tail feebly in acknowledgment of this remark, but seemed to have no real opinion on the matter.

Jack's thoughts kept running on these lines. He could not be quite sure whether or not he was frightened of ghosts.

I wouldn't mind seeing one from a distance, he thought, walking right through a wall. But I wouldn't want it to get too close. And I certainly wouldn't like it to walk through *me*.

He shuddered at the thought. Just then, Zero growled. Startled, Jack looked at him.

He must be telepathic! he thought. He's actually picked up my thoughts!

This was a very impressive String to add to Zero's Bow. Jack was delighted. He could hardly wait to tell the others—especially Tess.

"I always knew that you and I were close, old boy," he told Zero, "but I never knew that you could read my thoughts like that! You're brilliant!"

The snag was that Jack had now stopped thinking about ghosts, but Zero was still growling. He was lying in his customary boneless slump, but his eyes were open. He seemed to be looking at something beyond Jack. He was all the while giving a soft, throaty growl, and it seemed to Jack that his fur was beginning to stand up on end. He was sure it was, in places.

Jack was wondering whether he ought to whip suddenly round and try to catch a glimpse of whatever it was Zero was seeing, when the growling stopped. Zero gave a couple of final, grumpy snorts, and then his eyes shut again.

This left Jack not really knowing whether to claim that Zero had telepathic powers, or had sighted a phantom, even in broad daylight. Or, he wondered, both. In the end he decided on the latter. Nobody was much interested in Zero's personality or talents, whereas at present ghosts were much in vogue. It would be good for Zero to be one up on everyone else in this field.

He got up and went across the hall and into the kitchen, Zero at his heels. Jack could see at a glance that the available audience would not be very receptive. Mrs. Fosdyke was running back and forth with her eyes rolled upward, wielding a cobweb brush and doing a fair impression of someone unsuccessfully chasing butterflies. Jack had to step hastily out of her way to avoid collision. Mrs. Bagthorpe was scraping at the rusted boiler with one of Jack's camping knives and the noise produced was of such an excruciating order that Zero's ears went right down, and Jack even felt that his own might.

"Zero's just seen a ghost, Mother!" Jack told her loudly.

She looked up momentarily.

"Lovely, darling," she said, and carried on scraping. At this point Mrs. Fosdyke ran full tilt into Jack.

"Ooops!" she shrieked. "What are you doing there, under my feet? There's this whole house to be gone over from top to bottom, and I can't be doing with you and that dog under my feet. Ain't been cleaned for a hundred years, this place ain't, and won't be set to rights in five minutes. All of six weeks, it'll take, I shouldn't wonder. It's a marvel to me, the way foreigners live."

She sounded thoroughly happy at the prospect of spending the entire holiday exorcising every last speck of Welsh dust, every Welsh cobweb with its Welsh spider. She made it sound really fulfilling. Jack wondered gloomily whether she would find time to do any cooking. If not, he reflected, he preferred her as she had been before the goat charged her. At least then she had been ignorable.

He decided to wait for the return of the shopping party before making his announcement about Zero's psychic powers. He should have known better. Its members arrived laden with purchases and full of talk about how marvelous it had been to be back in civilization again. Also, they had been to a café and had enormous cream teas. Jack could have killed them.

I'll say it tonight, he thought, deciding on further postponement. At least then Uncle Parker will listen.

Mr. Bagthorpe had spent hundreds of pounds during the afternoon, he announced, and was in high good humor at the prospect of claiming it all back from Uncle Parker.

"Get your computer out and tot it up," he told Rosie. "It may eventually run into thousands, of course. Has that goat killed anyone while I've been gone?"

Something of a silence fell. No one had the remotest idea of the goat's whereabouts.

"You and that matted-up, pudding-footed hound of yours had better get out there and sniff it out," Mr. Bagthorpe told him. "Do it fast. It could still be in a killing mood. And it fetched its head a thumping great thwack against the wall. It's probably wandering about concussed. It'll be ready by now to go for the jugular."

He was, as usual, overdoing things. Mrs. Fosdyke, though by now thoroughly restored and filled with a kind of macabre glee at the colossal extent of the cleaning-up operations ahead, was nonetheless irritated by the high spirits of her old adversary. She chose this moment to make her revelation.

"I don't know about that *goat* being half conscious," she remarked quellingly. "*You* certainly was. In fact you was clean out."

Everyone looked at her expectantly, with the exception of Mr. Bagthorpe, who clenched and unclenched his fists.

" 'E fainted," she told them. "Fainted clean away. Frightened to death of that poor dumb animal."

This had not been Mrs. Fosdyke's original assessment of the goat. She had in fact watched from the kitchen window on the day it arrived and had chased Mr. Bagthorpe round the garden. She was also repelled by its smell, and the way it made puddles.

"I've never wondered much about how the Noahs went on in that Ark of theirs," she had confided to Mesdames Pye and Bates, "but I do now. I think about it all the time. All them animals! All them puddles! However did they go on? And not even any disinfectants, not in them days."

"I certainly show the goat a proper respect," Mr. Bagthorpe now coldly informed everyone, "as any sane man would. And as to my fainting—that is pure fantasy. I merely, being so sensitive and creative, felt a little dizzy on seeing my Writing Hand so severely...."

He trailed off, realizing his mistake.

"He thought that paint was blood!" Tess hooted. "He did a Florence Nightingale!"

"Or Gandhi," put in William, "or John Keats."

"You are *dim*, Father," Rosie told him, "you really are! Fancy mixing up oil paints with blood!"

"I 'ad to squeeze three clothsful of cold water over 'im," Mrs. Fosdyke told them smugly. "Good job I knew me drill, else 'e'd be lying there still."

"I think we must all start thinking about what we shall wear to go to the castle," Mrs. Bagthorpe now said, hoping to avert another all-out row. "We must heat pans of water in the kitchen and carry them up to the bathroom."

Little enthusiasm was shown for this suggestion.

"As they did in Victorian times," she added brightly. "It will give us all an interesting insight into the way people lived during that period."

"In Victorian times, Mother, there were servants," William pointed out. "There were kitchen maids, scullery maids, parlor maids, footmen, butlers—you name it!"

Mrs. Bagthorpe was temporarily floored by this truth, and hastily changed the subject.

"Go and find Daisy and your grandmother," she told Jack.

"And watch out for that blood-crazed goat!" Mr. Bagthorpe shouted after him.

Jack met the pair on their way back to the house. They had done enough dragon watching for the time being. The notorious Bagthorpe boredom threshold had been reached.

Billy Goat Gruff trotted sedately at Daisy's side, meek as a lamb, and certainly not looking, by any stretch of the imagination, blood-crazed. This, Jack realized, was going to infuriate his father.

"Hello, Zack!" called Daisy. "We finished looking for dragons now. We going to find ghosties."

"I should wait till it gets dark, Daisy," he advised. "And I bet the ghosts up at your castle are better than ours."

He fell into step with them, thinking he had better make sure they actually reached the house. They were likely at a moment's notice to go off at all kinds of unaccountable tangents.

"Grandma told me lots about dragons," Daisy informed him happily. "An' you'll never guess what! Dragons comes out of *eggs!*"

"Do they?" Jack asked Grandma.

"Certainly they do," she replied. "But these eggs are always very cleverly concealed. This is why one so rarely sees a dragon in captivity, or in a zoo."

"But wiv me being only *lickle,*" supplied Daisy, "I can get wight near the ground to *see* eggs! An' I got very bright eyes."

This last was certainly true. Daisy's eyes often did give the impression of being able to look in several directions at once. This was one of the more alarming things about her.

Jack led Grandma and Daisy back to the kitchen, so that his mission should be seen to have been accomplished.

They're not my responsibility now, he thought, not without relief. The Unholy Alliance represented an awesome responsibility for anyone.

"Just look at that goat!" cried Mrs. Fosdyke, with intent to infuriate. "Meek as a lamb, and good as gold!"

Mr. Bagthorpe glowered at her with murder in his heart. At that juncture, the goat made another of his puddles, and everyone sniggered, especially Mr. Bagthorpe.

Mrs. Fosdyke had not thought to live to see the day when she would take sides with the goat. She now felt herself forced into this all but untenable position.

She made a great show of not turning a hair.

"Them Parkers is too lax," she observed. "There's no use blaming a poor dumb animal. Anyone else'd 've got that goat trained by now. They do say people gets the pets they deserve. And that's what it looks like to me."

With which pious utterance she turned to her sink and commenced a purposeful rattle. Here she was at a disadvantage, because she had nowhere near the same scope for rattling and banging as she had at home. What with a shortage of pots, and the total absence of a draining board, there was a limit to what could be achieved in this line. She had to cut her rattle according to her sink.

ELEVEN

"Do not go stuffing yourselves with food, particularly of the disgustingly rich and unwholesome variety that Russell described," Mr. Bagthorpe warned his party before their departure for the castle. "I don't want you all falling asleep left and right by midnight."

"That cream tea you wolfed down was unwholesome, all right," William told him. "In fact, everybody might as well know that you had *two* cream teas."

"Oh, Henry!" exclaimed Mrs. Bagthorpe reprovingly.

Mr. Bagthorpe had done this partly because he was genuinely hungry, and partly because he wanted to fill himself right up. He would then, at the castle, be able to toy convincingly with his food, and spurn all that was offered to him. This seemed one of the few ways open to him to score over Uncle Parker, who was in the lap of luxury while the Bagthorpes were in a pigsty.

"And *why* can't we all fall asleep at midnight?" demanded Rosie.

"Because tonight we're getting down to business," he informed her. "We aren't here on a nonstop round of pleasure and idle self-indulgence."

"That, Henry, is a curious way to describe our holiday so far," Grandma said. "I should imagine that most inmates of Her Majesty's prisons are more cosseted than ourselves. I understand that many cells have carpets now, and curtains."

"Anyway, *what* business?" Rosie pressed.

"Tonight," he said, "once we have got this toadying social call out of the way, we are going to have a thoroughgoing Ghost Watch."

His offspring, who were already anticipating how gloriously drowsy and overfed they would be feeling in a few hours' time, groaned. Even Tess looked dubious. (She had not yet had the chance to rig up her Ghost Detecting Gear.)

"Don't you think that our *all* staying up to watch would be something of an overkill?" she asked.

Mr. Bagthorpe, however, was not the man to be afraid of the overkill.

"There are six apparitions," he replied, "there may even be more. I don't remember, and that goat consumed the list. We shall only be about one and a half persons per ghost."

"Pray do not include me, Henry," Grandma said. "At my age, I cannot be expected to spend all night in a deckchair straining my eyes to look for fictitious ghosts."

"Oooh, can I come, Uncle Bag?" squealed Daisy rapturously. "*I* want to catch a ghostie."

This optimistic request was turned down flat.

"You make sure you unload that unholy brat *and* her goat!" Mr. Bagthorpe hissed into Rosie's ear.

He then took William on one side, and warned him off telling Uncle Parker about his two cream teas. For one thing, this would spoil his strategy, and for another, it made him sound rather silly and schoolboyish, and would give Uncle Parker even more reason to look down on him.

At this point Mrs. Fosdyke made her entrance, looking brand new in her peach crepe. She had at first been uncertain whether or not to join the party. She finally decided in favor because she wanted to sample the opposition's food, to know what she was up against. Also, she had watched enough late night horror movies to be convinced that a Wailing Blue Light or Old Man Limping was at any rate in the cards. She harbored no ambitions to meet any of the bunch of apparitions described by Mr. Bagthorpe.

"Now!" exclaimed Mrs. Bagthorpe. "You *do* look nice, Mrs. Fosdyke. The five adults will travel up in the car, and you children can walk."

"And the goat," added her husband.

"Come on," William told the others, "let's get a start on them."

Jack left Zero in the kitchen, with orders to Stay and Guard.

"I know there's not a lot to guard," he told him, "but do it, anyway. Good boy!"

The younger Bagthorpes, plus Daisy and Billy Goat Gruff, set off at a gallop. The rest of the party went out to the car.

"I thought," remarked Grandma, as she seated herself next to Mrs. Fosdyke in the back seat, "I thought, Laura, that you said *five* adults. There appear to be only four of us."

"Oh—my heavens! Father!" Mrs. Bagthorpe, aghast, leaped out of the driving seat and stood in the overgrown drive looking helplessly about her.

They had mislaid Grandpa.

There are no doubt many families who have never in their history mislaid one of their founder members. The Bagthorpes, however, were not as others. They tended to go ruthlessly along their own tracks, looking to neither left nor right. In this instance, however, there was some excuse for their seemingly heartless oversight.

Grandpa, for most of the time, was *in* the family, and yet not *of* it. He pursued his peaceful, blameless existence parallel with the rest of the Bagthorpes, but hardly ever overlapping. He was the still heart at the center of the whirlwind.

Be this as it may, Mrs. Bagthorpe, at least, was stricken with remorse, even though it was her husband's father, and not her own, who had been mislaid.

"Father!" she called, wheeling about as though she half expected him to materialize up a tree. "Father!"

Mr. Bagthorpe wrenched open his own door and climbed out.

"There is no use your standing there bleating, Laura," he told her. "Are you *wandering*? Have you taken leave of your senses? Father is *deaf*. He has been deaf this past thirty years."

"Oh, yes—of course," she faltered.

None of the many thousands of readers of Stella Bright (Mrs. Bagthorpe's pseudonym as Agony Aunt in the magazine) would have been impressed by her wisdom, calm assurance and down-to-earth common sense could they have seen her now. They would certainly not have been inclined to write off to her about their own Problems.

"What shall we do?" she asked lamely. "Whatever are we to do?"

"Alfred went fishing," Grandma informed them from the back seat of the car, where she was still arranging her skirts. "He went in search of a stream, a pool." Here, with immaculate timing, she paused. "He cannot, of course, swim."

"Oh, dear! Oh, dear!" cried Mrs. Bagthorpe, going into a downward spiral as had been intended.

"Take a few deep breaths," her husband advised her. "Get a grip on yourself, Laura."

"Mr. Bagthorpe Senior," opined Mrs. Fosdyke, herself remaining seated, " 'as got a bit of sense. Not like some others. He'll be out there fishing somewhere, as 'appy as Larry."

On this occasion, *she* sounded rather like Stella Bright.

"You may or may not be right, Mrs. Fosdyke," Grandma

said. "But what is disgraceful is that you, Henry, should have totally overlooked your own father. It was he who gave you life."

"How about you, then?" he countered. "*You'd* clean forgotten him. He's your husband."

"That is hardly the same thing," she told him. "The tie between man and wife cannot be compared with that between father and son. That, Henry, is a sacred tie, a *blood* bond."

(Grandma often made this kind of distinction between various relationships, when it suited her book.)

"Bilge, Mother!" Mr. Bagthorpe snapped. Nobody would have supposed the blood bond between himself and his mother to be very sacred, at this point in time.

"What I suggest," continued Grandma, "is that the rest of us drive on up to the castle, and that you, Henry, remain here and search for your father."

Mr. Bagthorpe, despite his show of reluctance to go to the castle at all, was not enamored of this idea. He had, in his breast pocket, a sizeable bill, worked out by Rosie's computer, that he intended to present to Uncle Parker at the point where it was most likely to spoil his meal.

"I do not think Father would wish to be treated like a child," he said. "We will simply leave a note, telling him to come up and join us."

"I have said all that I intend to say on the subject," announced Grandma. "It is to be hoped that the evening does not end with the police dredging pools."

Mrs. Bagthorpe then feebly volunteered to remain behind herself, but this offer was vetoed by her husband.

"It would be ungracious," he told her.

"Oh, dear—I suppose it would." Mrs. Bagthorpe really did have Problems. Hardly any of the readers who wrote to her column had Problems of such magnitude and frequency as her own.

In the end, she unlocked the house door, wrote a note for Grandpa and left it on the kitchen table, then re-emerged, locking the door again behind her. Nobody noticed this, or if they did, they did not remark on it. The truth was that *none* of the Bagthorpes had a cool head in an emergency.

"I'm afraid that my evening is quite spoiled," she sighed, as she drove off.

"Bilge, Laura," he told her. "Father has lived to his present ripe age without your nannying him, and will probably outlive us all."

The journey took less than two minutes.

"Just look at *that!*" exclaimed Mr. Bagthorpe in disgust as they rolled into the castle grounds and over the drawbridge. "There's no wonder that man shies off reading the *Guardian!*"

"Russell has such style," remarked Grandma. "Such elegance!"

Mrs. Bagthorpe drove round to the car park, where her husband again had a speech to make about corrupt, materialistic values.

"Ye gods!" he exclaimed, looking about him at the gleaming ranks of Rollses, Jaguars, Austin-Healeys, Porsches and Aston Martins. "Just look at that lot! If that lot was all sold off tomorrow at auction, the problems of the Third World would be solved for a decade!"

As the Bagthorpes disembarked from their own car (which was four years old and had been chosen purely for reasons of utility and economy), yet another Bentley glided smoothly in and parked beside them. Mr. Bagthorpe gave its innocent occupants a glare of such ferocity that they must have spent the rest of the evening wondering which old enemy of theirs he was, and trying to place him.

As the party rounded the path to the front entrance they were hailed from above, and saw the others waving from a terrace.

"All right, all right!" Mr. Bagthorpe shouted tetchily in response to their cries of welcome. "We're coming! Give us a chance!"

There were noisy and effusive greetings as the two parties met. The goat, Jack noted, was tethered to a balustrade by a pink silk ribbon, and was wearing his full complement of bows and bells. Other people were seated on the terrace sipping their drinks and conversing in low murmurs.

"Are you quite recovered from your journey, Celia dear?" inquired Mrs. Bagthorpe.

Aunt Celia seemed at first not to hear this. She was gazing, lips slightly parted, into the gathering dusk over the woods and the mountains beyond. She was dressed more like a waterfall than ever—possibly as a Welsh cataract. When Mrs. Bagthorpe repeated her inquiry, she seemed, with an effort, to pull herself away from whatever vision she was having.

"I long only to lay down the burden of humanity," she said dreamily. "I long to dwell in mountain solitudes, writing immortal verse, and communing with nature."

Mrs. Bagthorpe was somewhat nonplused by this response to a question about car sickness. It was the kind of remark that is difficult to follow.

"It *is* beautiful," she agreed, advancing to the balustrade (though giving the goat a wide berth), "and what a view!"

"We can see your pad, look, down below," Uncle Parker told her. "Look—see there—that's the roof among the trees."

This aerial view of *Ty Cilion Duon* was even less prepossessing than on ground level. The state of the roof was parlous. When the Welsh rain began, there would be trouble.

"Just look at that!" exclaimed Mrs. Fosdyke, peering past them. "Just look at them great 'oles in the roof!"

Jack saw that other people were also glancing down with interest at this shaming sight. Mr. Bagthorpe was fuming. It was not enough, it seemed, for Uncle Parker to look down on him metaphorically, he had to do so literally as well.

"Mummy! Mummy!" squealed Daisy, tugging at one of Aunt Celia's fronds. (Daisy herself was got up, as usual, in all manner of furbelows. Mr. Bagthorpe often said she looked like a cross between Bo Peep and a lopped-off maypole.) At first, she received no response. Aunt Celia was off on her own somewhere again. Daisy, however, was nothing if not persistent.

"Mummy!" she squealed, in an even more piercing register. "What's a hovel?"

At this point a waiter mercifully appeared bearing menus. His manner seemed somewhat cool, and it occurred to Mr. Bagthorpe that while Uncle Parker might know the owner of the castle, this was no guarantee that the staff would gladly embrace Daisy and her goat.

Mr. Bagthorpe enjoyed studying the menu. His eye roamed down it, looking for the most expensive items. He would taste each course, he thought, and then push away the plate. This way, Uncle Parker would at a stroke be snubbed and out of pocket.

On the other hand, if he ordered the avocado and prawns he might be tempted to eat it, despite his earlier cream tea double.

I'll pick the Chef's Pâté, he decided. Then, when I don't eat it, it'll prove the chef's no good.

He was not, then, so much selecting a menu as planning a strategy of war.

From his point of view the meal went swimmingly. He pushed away his pâté after only a single mouthful. He barely touched his Tournedos Rossini.

"Do you have such a commodity as a Doggy Bag?" he asked the head waiter in ringing tones. This idea had only just occurred to him, and he considered it a master stroke. Many heads were turned in his direction.

Crikey! thought Jack, amazed. He *does* like Zero, even if he pretends not to!

While the others were eating, Mr. Bagthorpe made long and difficult mental calculations of the eventual size of Uncle Parker's bill. While doing so, he took copious swigs of his wine (which he had decided to pretend was tolerable) and another bottle was ordered. He was, then, in high good humor when the party adjourned to the terrace for coffee and liqueurs.

I'll give it five minutes, he thought, and then present him with the bill for this afternoon's little lot. That, with the bill for this, should run nicely into four figures.

The evening was calm and balmy. The terrace was softly lit. Far away below came the faint notes of a police siren. It was as if it came from another world. As the Bagthorpes sat there, pleasantly wined and dined (and, in one or two cases, gorged), there was a momentary calm and relaxation about them. They might almost have been taken for any other ordinary family on an evening out.

Coffee and mints were distributed. Mrs. Fosdyke knocked

back her apricot brandy (probably chosen as a near match for her outfit) at a single gulp.

"Where's Grandpa?" asked Jack suddenly.

"He went fishing," Mrs. Bagthorpe replied swiftly, before Grandma could get her oar in. "He didn't get back in time."

"He probably wouldn't have come anyway," Mr. Bagthorpe said. "Like myself, he is very unworldly." He paused. "As opposed, of course, to *other*worldly, which is something else again," he added pointedly, looking at Aunt Celia.

She was gazing down below, as one hypnotized. Her lips were moving. Jack, with no real belief that he would see what *she* could see, followed the direction of her gaze.

"Crikey!" he exclaimed. "Look!"

They all did so. There, away down below at *Ty Cilion Duon*, was a brilliant blue light, winking and flashing among the trees.

"By Jove!" exclaimed Uncle Parker. "A police raid! Were you expecting one, Henry?"

TWELVE

"Father!" exclaimed Mrs. Bagthorpe faintly.

"Spot of bother, it would seem," agreed Uncle Parker.

"It's the fuzz!" yelled William. "Come on—let's go!"

The party broke up in disorder. As they scattered, other diners went crowding to the balustrade, pointing and exclaiming.

The younger Bagthorpes, quite neglecting to thank their host, went pell-mell over the drawbridge and down the hill. In the car park, Mrs. Bagthorpe's nerveless fingers fumbled on the dashboard.

"Oh, dear, oh, dear!" she sobbed.

"There is no use your getting in a state now, Laura," Grandma told her. "It is too late. Any harm has already been done."

"I don't know, I really don't," came Mrs. Fosdyke's lugubrious voice from the darkness. "Only been 'ere a day, and mixed up with the police already!"

"If Mohammed won't go to the mountain, the mountain must come to Mohammed," remarked Mr. Bagthorpe enigmatically—and inaccurately.

"Meaning what, exactly, Henry?" inquired Grandma.

"Meaning," he replied, "that I was going to have a word with the police anyway, about that trickster Jones."

(He did not, of course, know this, but one of the officers was related to this elusive gentleman, and was later able to give him warning that Mr. Bagthorpe was after him.)

Mrs. Bagthorpe was so engaged with a mental picture of Grandpa laid out on a stretcher and covered with a white sheet that she narrowly missed running over a member of her own family, thus rendering *him* a candidate for the police mortuary.

"Hell's bells, Laura!" said Mr. Bagthorpe. "That was William you nearly winged. Are you bent on slaughtering the whole family? Slow *down!*"

The car party arrived marginally before the pedestrians. As the car drew up behind the police car, its blue light still flashing, the head lamps picked out two uniformed officers, standing by the front door and apparently in deep consultation. Of Grandpa there was no sign.

Mrs. Bagthorpe switched off the engine. She sat for a moment, stunned, got out of the car—and fainted.

Afterward, Mr. Bagthorpe used this a lot as ammunition.

"We all have different ways of coping with reality," he would say. "When things get tough, some of us sneeze—and some of us, of course, faint. The archetypal copout."

At the time of her swooning, the pedestrian contingent came hurtling up and barely missed tripping over their prostrate parent. Mrs. Fosdyke scrambled out of the back seat and immediately went into her St. John's Ambulance routine.

"Stand back, stand back!" she ordered, and this despite the fact that no one was anywhere near the patient, let alone hanging anxiously over her. "Give her air!"

There was a plethora of this commodity, but a shortage, unfortunately, of cloths and cold water. Mrs. Fosdyke slapped her employer's cheeks several times, but with no response.

"Improvise . . . ," she muttered. "Improvise. . . ."

Mrs. Fosdyke as a personality was a stranger to improvisation. She ran through her life like a tram on rails. This word, however, had lodged in her mind from her evening classes, and now, like grit in the oyster, it brought forth its pearl.

Scanning rapidly about, her eye fell on a water butt by the house. She tugged from the shoulders of her unconscious patient a crocheted shawl, and ran over to the butt.

The deluge of water that poured from this woolen article when squeezed would probably have reversed a cardiac arrest. It certainly brought Mrs. Bagthorpe to with a vengeance. She shot to her feet twice as fast as she could have done under ordinary circumstances.

"What's happening?" she cried urgently. "Where am I? What is that blue light?"

She received no reply to any of these queries. Mrs. Fosdyke had now lost all interest in her resuscitated patient, and was listening, agog, to the saga being unfolded by the police officers.

The whole story was not finally pieced together until much later, but what it amounted to was this.

Grandpa had set off in search of fishing. He had had to go a fair way before finding anything promising. He then settled himself by the pool with happy anticipation. Once he got staring at the surface of the water, he lapsed into much the same state of beatific peace as that produced by gazing at the television screen (with or without pictures).

The hours slid by, then, in a state of happy hypnosis. The light began to fail. He might have stayed on, even then, had he not begun to feel nagging pangs of hunger. Normally when he went on a fishing expedition, Mrs. Fosdyke would put him up an excellent picnic, with chicken drumsticks and his favorite stuffed eggs. Grandpa was certainly unworldly, but he did have to eat in order to stay alive, and so he reluctantly packed his gear and made off in the direction of where he thought his temporary home was. His catch was small, because the goat and Mr. Bagthorpe had between them left him seriously short of baits and line. As he was preparing to leave, his foot caught on a root and he fell sideways into the pool. (Grandma later claimed that this proved that she was psychic. She had foretold this, she said.)

The pool was mercifully shallow at the edge, but the water was naturally as wet as if it had been the Atlantic Ocean. Grandpa emerged dripping, and with water in his hearing aid.

He then set off as fast as he could, with discomfort now an added incentive to hunger. His sense of direction had never been good. Grandma often told the story of how, in their youth, they had started off for a holiday in Brittany and ended up in Spain. This would not have been so bad if they had not both spent the previous winter taking very expensive lessons in French conversation. This experience must have sown the seeds (though he was only six at the time) of Mr. Bagthorpe's xenophobia.

Grandpa, then, completely overshot *Ty Cilion Duon*, but did, eventually, land up in Llosilly itself. By now the light had almost gone. He stood in the main street, looking bewilderedly about him and shivering a little in his wet clothes. There he was discovered by a party of locals on their way to The Welsh Harp. Struck by the appearance of this dripping stranger in their midst, they asked if they could be of any assistance. Grandpa, who could hear not a word they said because of the waterlogged hearing aid, merely nodded and beamed.

Now the point about Grandpa was that he had a very nice face. He had the kind of face that you could warm to even if he had just run into the back of your car. People took to him instantly. He was alone in this of the Bagthorpe clan (with the possible exception of Jack).

After a conference, the locals decided to take him to the police house. There, they argued, he would at least be given a hot drink, and possibly even a change of clothing. Also, it was part of the police's duty to deal with missing persons. (Not that Grandpa exactly fell into that category. He was present—it was his family who were missing.)

Grandpa had not taken much notice of his new surroundings at *Ty Cilion Duon*, nor did he even know the name of the house. He had been too taken up by his television snowstorm. He was not able to give the policeman any real clues. When, however, he gave his name as Bagthorpe, there was an instant reaction from the party who had brought him in. (Mrs. Bagthorpe had written a check at the Village Stores. She did not carry about the kind of money needed to pay for making a clean sweep of the shop's disinfectants and cleaning materials.)

"There's a rum English bloke staying up there," one of the locals told the policeman. "Cracked, they reckon."

"Been in The Welsh Harp, they say," supplied another. "Spying."

"After Dai Jones he is, see."

"What kind of man is it leaves his aged father dripping wet in the street, after dark?"

"Terrible."

"Seems a lovely old gentleman, too."

Here Grandpa had reappeared, dressed in some old clothes of Constable Griffith's, and looking very happy to be dry again.

"I reckon you should get him taken back there in a car, Gareth," advised one of the constable's friends. "Give the police a chance, then, it would, to see what's going on there."

"And let that Bagthorpe fellow know the police have got their eye on him."

This policy was generally agreed upon, and the constable accordingly telephoned for a squad car. Grandpa's hearing aid was improving by the minute, as it generally did when he was with strangers, and when he was finally made to understand that he was to be taken home in a police car, it became quite miraculously effective.

One of Grandpa's unfulfilled ambitions was to ride in a police car with the blue light flashing. He had never confided this to any of his family. There seemed little point. The Bagthorpes were interested only in their own unfulfilled ambitions. As he grew older, Grandpa had come sadly to accept that this particular ambition never would be fulfilled now. It had never really been in the cards. People who travel in police cars with the blue light flashing have usually committed a serious offense, and are sitting in the back handcuffed to an officer. Grandpa was not the murdering sort. The only things he went in for killing were wasps (and even this he tried to do humanely, with a swift blow from a rolled up copy of the *Guardian*).

Now, however, he saw his chance. He confided his long-held yearning to his sympathetic audience, and they were unanimous in agreeing that he should be indulged in this whim.

"Poor old gentleman. Why has he not been reported missing? Where are his family, then?"

"Scare the living daylights out of them, when they see that blue light. Serve them right, too."

When the officers arrived in the patrol car, the situation was explained to them.

"No problem," said the driver. "Blue light flashing it is, then. See if we can't manage a quick burst of the old siren, too. Come along, then, Grandad."

So it was that when all parties converged on *Ty Cilion Duon*, the only genuinely happy person present was Grandpa (except possibly Grandma, who adored anything to do with the police). He sat in the back seat throughout the confrontation that followed, watching, enchanted, the steady play of blue light flickering about him. This probably, apart from anything else, helped his withdrawal symptoms after the loss of his television.

Mr. Bagthorpe, having once ascertained that Grandpa was alive and well and in the back seat of the squad car, started shouting almost immediately. He believed attack always to be the best form of defense. He accused the police of unprofessional excess of zeal.

"He was only half a mile away from *home*, for crying out loud," he told them. "We come home and find half the Welsh police force trespassing on our property, and blue lights flashing left and right. Don't you think you are overreacting?"

"Been out, then, had you, sir?" asked Officer One.

"We have had a very enjoyable evening up at the castle," Grandma told him. "I told Henry that he should stay behind and look for his father. He might easily have been drowned."

"Certainly he might, madam," agreed Officer Two. "Is that a body over there?"

"It's only Mother," William told him.

At this point Mrs. Fosdyke squeezed her wooly shawl, and Mrs. Bagthorpe, now dripping herself like a Welsh cataract, was revived and able to join in the Inquiry.

On being assured that Grandpa was not drowned, she

clasped her hands, and exclaimed, "Thank heaven! Thank heaven!"

"I don't know about that, madam," said Officer One. "It certainly doesn't appear to be thanks to any of you."

"Seems an odd way to carry on, going off and leaving an old gentleman dripping wet and locked out in the dark," added Officer Two.

"Nonsense," she returned. "A note was left for him on the kitchen table."

"We shall have to check on that, madam," he told her. "First, we need to effect an entry."

"Try turning the knob," advised Mr. Bagthorpe with heavy sarcasm.

"Perhaps, sir, you would like to do so," suggested One.

Mr. Bagthorpe strode forward and wrenched at the knob. He rattled hard. The door was locked. This made him feel extremely silly.

"Laura," he gritted, "you locked the door!"

"Oh—oh, dear!" faltered Mrs. Bagthorpe. She looked at the officers and met their condemnatory stares. She drew herself up, dripping steadily.

"I—I am a magistrate," she informed them. "A Justice of the Peace."

"Really, madam?" said Two politely.

"We surveyed the property for a means of entry," said One, "but we didn't like the sound of the dog."

"Zero!" exclaimed Jack, overjoyed.

"Very nasty snarl," the officer continued.

"Snarl?" echoed Mr. Bagthorpe disbelievingly. "Did you say *snarl*?"

"I set him to Guard, Father," Jack told him happily. He

could hardly believe it himself. He had not known that Zero really knew what the word Guard meant. In the past, he had sometimes been told to Guard, but no one really knew whether he did this or not. But now they had proof, from two police officers, that Zero was a first-class guard dog with a terrifying snarl. The evidence was unimpeachable—even Mr. Bagthorpe would not be able to discount it later.

It's *another* String to his Bow! he thought. That's two more Strings, in a single day!

As the rest of the Bagthorpes stood reeling under this testament to Zero, a long, high-pitched howl was heard. Zero, shut in the kitchen at the rear of the house, evidently wished to be let out. Simultaneously there came the usual spurting of gravel that heralded the arrival of Uncle Parker. He narrowly missed careering into the Bagthorpes' car. Had he come a few minutes earlier, he would probably have run over the unconscious Mrs. Bagthorpe.

"Oooh!" squealed Daisy Parker's voice. "Come on, Billy Goat Gruff!"

The two officers stared incredulously as she climbed out, tugging the goat behind her. They had enough bells between them to furnish an entire Alpine herd.

"Look at the winky light!" Daisy told her pet. "It's like when Daddy drives too fast!"

"Ha!" exclaimed Mr. Bagthorpe. "Hear that, Russell? Hear that, you two?"

"Hullo again, all," Uncle Parker greeted them affably. "Good evening, officers."

"What are you doing down here?" demanded Mr. Bagthorpe.

"Celia sent me," he replied. "Wouldn't have closed her eyes

all night, otherwise. My word, Henry, it doesn't take *you* long to rouse the neighborhood, does it? Hallo, Laura—fallen into something, have you?"

"I squoze her shawl over her," Mrs. Fosdyke informed him. "Had to, see. It was improvising."

Uncle Parker was clearly puzzled by this explanation, but did not pursue his inquiry. He knew all too well Mrs. Fosdyke's tendency to ramble on.

"Watch that goat," Mr. Bagthorpe warned the policemen. "You could end up impaled on its horns. It's a killer."

"Laura," said Grandma, "unlock the door and let us go in and continue our conversation there. And I daresay these two kind officers would welcome a cup of tea."

She made this invitation partly to enrage Mr. Bagthorpe and partly because she was very interested in police procedure. She was something of a buff on the subject.

"That's most kind, madam, thank you," replied Officer One.

He knew as well as she knew, and as well as Mr. Bagthorpe knew, for that matter, that he could not enter the premises unless invited, given the absence of a warrant. He already had the strong impression that sooner, rather than later, a warrant, or even several warrants, would be issued. He smiled, feeling himself to be one up on the Bagthorpes. He should, he later realized, have checked on their police records first. As it was, he went in like a lamb to the slaughter.

THIRTEEN

Once the Bagthorpes were sitting round in the kitchen with the police officers, drinking countless cups of tea and holding a very badly run Inquiry, the place really did begin to seem like home.

"Nice place you've got here," remarked Officer One. (He it was who was related to the missing Mr. Jones.)

"Think so, do you?" said Mr. Bagthorpe. "Are you by any chance blind?"

"Blind, sir?" echoed the officer, straightfaced, trying not to look at either his colleague or the *Titanic* boiler.

"Like the stainless steel sink, do you?" asked Mr. Bagthorpe sardonically. "And the latest split-level cooker, and the fridge?"

"And the working surfaces," added Mrs. Fosdyke automatically.

The list of missing kitchen equipment was now indelibly printed on her mind. From that time onward, all she needed was a trigger word, and she would recite the whole list, in a flat, mechanical voice, rather like that of a Speak Your Weight machine, or an announcer at an airport.

"Holiday home, though, isn't it?" said Officer Two. "Got to do a bit of mucking in on holiday, haven't you?"

"Why, you took the place, after all, Henry," interposed Uncle Parker. "Toughening up, character-training and all that."

There were times when Mr. Bagthorpe did genuinely feel

like murdering Uncle Parker. Thanks to him, he was now on the horns of a dilemma. If he kept up his pretense that he had gone to some lengths to procure so squalid a place in order to improve his family's characters, then he could make no complaint about misrepresentation to the police. On the other hand, if he pitched straight in about the state of the house, and demanded Jones's arrest and his own money back, then Uncle Parker would begin to wear that certain smile. Mr. Bagthorpe thought he had detected hints of it already.

Mr. Bagthorpe thought fast.

"I shall be coming round to the station to make a formal complaint in the morning," he informed the pair. "I intend to sue Mr. Jones."

"And on what grounds will that be, sir?" asked One.

"I do not intend to go into sordid details now," he replied. "But it will be under the Trades Descriptions Act."

"There are supposed to be ghosts here, you see," Rosie explained. "Dozens of them. And we haven't seen a single one. None of us has."

Here Jack had his golden cue.

"Zero has," he said.

All eyes turned to him, and then to Zero, who was now lying by him in his usual slump, like sculpted dough.

"This afternoon," he explained. "In the sitting room. He did a sort of little growl in his throat, and looked at something straight behind me. And his fur stood up on end—at least, it did in places."

"*That* testimony will not stand up in court," Mr. Bagthorpe told him.

"I expect he had caught a glimpse of darling Thomas the Second," Grandma said. "For some unaccountable reason, none of you appears to be very fond of him—though you do not, of course, growl."

It was true that none of the Bagthorpes, including Zero, cared for Grandma's latest protégé, but the reasons for this were by no means unaccountable. When Thomas the Second was a kitten, Grandma and Daisy had put him through a very intensive training, following, Mr. Bagthorpe maintained, the methods used by terrorists with new recruits. Most people present had been bitten by him at least once, and all of them had been severely scratched—including Zero.

Jack had not thought of this. He began to wish he had kept quiet about Zero's psychic powers.

If I cry "Wolf!" he thought, people won't believe it when he actually *does* see his first ghost.

"If that hound of yours had anything about him," Mr. Bagthorpe told Jack, "he'd go for that malevolent ginger brute and put paid to him. For two pins, I'd do it myself."

"I hope that you have made a note of that, officers," Grandma told the police. "You really must be careful, Henry, what threats you make in front of witnesses."

"It certainly is a 'orrible cat," observed Mr. Fosdyke, "but no one should go threatening 'arm to dumb creatures. And you should've seen 'im this afternoon, with that goat."

"What exactly *was* the incident, madam?" asked Two.

The Bagthorpes were turning out to be even more interesting than he had thought.

"*You* never saw its like," Mrs. Fosdyke told him with utter conviction. She took a deep breath and prepared to launch into her account.

Nobody else wanted to hear this. It had all happened hours ago and was, so far as they were concerned, stale news. Mr.

Bagthorpe wanted to hear it least of all. Fortunately, mention of the goat incident reminded him of the bill in his breast pocket, still unpresented.

"I'm glad the goat came up," he said. "I didn't give it to you earlier, Russell, for fear of putting you off your food. But here is the bill for the replacement of the stuff that goat trampled on and put its hoofs through."

He took out the bill and presented it.

"It's not complete yet, I may as well warn you. I hope you're making a note of this," he added, to the police officers.

Uncle Parker glanced at the bill and raised his eyebrows slightly.

"By Jove!" he exclaimed pleasantly. "One might almost suppose that the goat had written off your car, Henry. Was all this stuff insured?"

"Thanks to you and your infernal daughter," Mr. Bagthorpe replied, "over the months my insurance premiums have risen to a level I can scarcely afford. I would have credited you, Russell, with enough sense to take out a large and comprehensive policy the moment that goat set hoof in your house."

The officers were witnessing this exchange rather in the manner of spectators at Wimbledon during a rally, but others, notably Grandma, were tiring of this two-cornered fight.

"My son," she told the officers, "has for years been waging relentless war on a child scarcely out of the nursery."

"Really, madam?" said Two, bewildered by this sudden turn.

"I think that now you are here you should make a note of that, too," she continued. "If you wish, I am quite prepared to make a sworn statement to that effect."

"And me," piped up Rosie. "Father's really horrible to poor little Daisy. She's sweet."

For this piece of treachery she was rewarded by a murderous glare from Mr. Bagthorpe.

"Would that be the child in question?" inquired Officer One, indicating Daisy. She was seated on the floor, rummaging through Mrs. Fosdyke's Portable Pantry. No one could even begin to guess what she was looking for. No one had to date come anywhere near working out the way Daisy's mind worked.

" 'Ere!" said Mrs. Fosdyke sharply. "Let my things alone!"

"You see?" Grandma appealed to the officers. "It almost amounts to a conspiracy against the child. Her every innocent action is interpreted as a crime."

"That child," Mr. Bagthorpe told them, "has cost myself and her father tens of thousands of pounds in the last few months alone. We have also, on occasion, all narrowly missed losing our lives. In my opinion, you should open a file on her— fast."

The two policemen laughed politely at what they took to be Mr. Bagthorpe's little joke.

"Rather early days for you to expect to see any apparitions, don't you think, Henry?" said Uncle Parker, neatly drawing the fire off Daisy. "After all, you've got to give the place a chance to settle down."

"What in heaven's name are you burbling about?" demanded Mr. Bagthorpe, staring.

"Vibrations," explained Uncle Parker. "You lot descending on the place yesterday must have given the vibrations a pretty good shake-up. Ghosts are sensitive to that kind of thing. You, of all people, must see that, Henry."

"You know nothing about vibrations," Mr. Bagthorpe told

him, nettled that Uncle Parker should start lecturing on a subject on which he himself claimed to be an authority. "None of you do. If there are any ghosts around here, *I* shall see them. And if there are not, then I shall go for Jones under the Trades Descriptions Act."

"Difficult, I should have thought," drawled Uncle Parker.

"What d'you mean, difficult?" Mr. Bagthorpe returned. "It'll be cut and dried. Open and shut."

"Will you bring the Trades Descriptions Board down here for a night or two, to see for themselves?" inquired Uncle Parker.

While things were warming up between the two of them, the two policemen exchanged looks.

"Not seen anything yet, then, sir?" asked Number One. "You surprise me."

"Brave man to stop here at all," put in Number Two. "Darned if I would."

"It is true, then!" cried Tess ecstatically. "It really *is* haunted!"

"You keep out of it," her father told her curtly. "We're talking about facts now, not half-baked notions."

"I know more about the paranormal than any of you," Tess replied. "And that's another thing, Uncle Park. I've put in claims for my oboe, and my tape recorder that Billy Goat Gruff smashed, but what about my pyramids?"

At this, the police officers started looking bewildered. They had thought they were on firm ground when ghosts were under discussion, but now they were at sea again.

"By 'pyramids'," ventured Two tentatively, "do we mean —pyramids?"

"I know they were only homemade," continued Tess, "and

possibly not of any great monetary value per se. But they were an indispensable part of my experiments. It is extremely exacting work, the dimensions have to be absolutely to scale for mummification to occur. I'm afraid I shall have to put in an estimated claim, based on how long it will take me to reconstruct them."

"Well, yes, I can see that," Uncle Parker conceded. "I think I more or less get your drift. Bang in a claim then, Tess."

"Pyramids," Number Two repeated, more or less to himself. "Pyramids."

"She uses 'em to put dead mice under," Mr. Bagthorpe told him.

"I see." Two, dazed, made a note.

"About these ghosts," said One, loudly, determined to bring discussion back to earth. "This house, sir, is definitely haunted."

"It *is*?" exclaimed Mr. Bagthorpe. This sounded promising, coming from an officer of the law. He was not to know that Jones was the officer's relative.

"Oh, definitely."

"What by?" Mr. Bagthorpe demanded.

One hesitated.

"A Wailing Blue Light," said Jack.

"And an Old Man Limping," supplied William.

"Exactly," nodded One. "There's none in these parts'd care to come here after dark." He then ill-advisedly attempted a quip. "Though I daresay you might scare *them* as much as the other way round!"

This fell on stony ground. No one laughed, or even smiled. Grandma fixed him with a riveting look.

"This is not a laughing matter, constable," she told him sternly.

This was mainly to cover up her own nervousness. If an officer of the law said that the place was haunted, then she was inclined to believe him. She had begun to feel that Tess's hypnotism was wearing off again.

"Perhaps I might make a suggestion?" said Uncle Parker mildly.

"We'd rather you didn't," Mr. Bagthorpe told him rudely.

"It seems to me," continued Uncle Parker, "now that we are all gathered together, and the time, as you will observe, is approaching the witching hour, we might do a little serious research."

He paused.

"Sir?" prompted Two, who had put him down as one of the saner members of the family.

"We have with us," Uncle Parker said, "a prime example of a highly tuned man. A man who picks up vibrations as a magnet picks up filings, or a cat fleas. Yourself, of course, Henry."

While Mr. Bagthorpe was trying to work out whether or not this was a compliment, and if so, how to react to it, Uncle Parker went on.

"We also," he said, "have with us men of faultless and irreproachable character. Men of insight, wisdom and understanding. Men of the highest caliber, the noblest breed. Yourselves, gentlemen."

Here he bowed toward the bewildered One and Two. (Uncle Parker had a long history of buttering up police officers, and was by now an expert in this field. He had to be, given the way he drove his car.)

"So what?" said William.

"So we will turn out the lights," Uncle Parker said, "and

sit absolutely still, as at a séance, and we will await a mani-
festation."

There now fell one of those all too rare silences in the Bagthorpe menage.

"W-will we hold hands?" quavered Rosie at last.

"Certainly not!" snapped Mr. Bagthorpe, who happened to
be standing next to Mrs. Fosdyke.

"It is rather a splendid idea, Russell," Mrs. Bagthorpe told
him gamely. "Very bold and imaginative." She was still somewhat in a state of shock, though drying out nicely.

"After all, even before we went out you said we were going
to have a Ghost Watch," Tess reminded her father.

"What do you say, officers?" asked Uncle Parker. "Think
what a scoop it would be, if something popped up!"

"I think that you are confusing them with newspapermen,"
Mr. Bagthorpe told him. "I also think that your vibrations
would be enough to scare off any ghost, however seasoned."

"I think it's a good idea," Jack said. He still believed in
Zero's fur. If it stood up on end, he would have police witnesses.

"Don't start until I get back!" Rosie cried, and ran off to
fetch her camera and flash equipment.

"She will not obtain a photograph with *her* camera," Tess
informed the others. "Psychic energy and ectoplasm can only
be registered by Kirlean photography."

The two policemen were holding a whispered conference.
It was definitely no part of their duties to take part in im-
promptu séances. On the other hand, they argued, it could be
valuable evidence if Mr. Bagthorpe ever needed to be proved
mad. Also, it would add weight to their claim that the house
was known to be haunted if they showed confidence that such

a séance was worthwhile. Beyond these pragmatic considerations, both officers, without even knowing it, were for the time being spellbound by the sheer glamour of the Bagthorpes, their cool, their confidence, their lack of resemblance to any other human beings they had ever encountered.

"We can't spare long, I'm afraid," One announced at last. "But we are prepared to take part in the investigation."

"It may provide valuable evidence," added Two—though he did not specify of what.

Mrs. Fosdyke was not sure that she wished to take part in any such foolhardy experiment. She was well aware of the dangers of tinkering with the supernatural. Corpses sucked dry of blood were a commonplace, in her experience. Nor did she believe that the presence of the two police officers was adequate protection against malevolent invisible powers. All too often, such people were the first to go. On the other hand, if she declined to participate, then she would be all by herself in another part of the house. This prospect did not greatly appeal to her, either.

Pity I ain't got a cross hung round my neck, she thought morosely. Though I could keep my fingers crossed, I suppose.

As she thought along these lines, vague memories stirred. Mrs. Fosdyke's memory was retentive, but fragmented. She could not for the life of her think whether drawing a pentagon and standing inside it was meant to ward off the devil, or to invoke him. Then a small, solitary fact floated to the surface.

"Garlic!" she exclaimed.

She scuttled over to her Portable Pantry and commenced a feverish scrabbling among its contents. This was not easy. What she had there, so great was her mistrust of Abroad, was more or less a Portable Supermarket.

She finally located the greengrocery department just as

Rosie returned with her camera and the rest were forming themselves into a ring, ready to start.

"There!" she cried triumphantly, flourishing her string of garlic.

"What does she mean by whirling that garlic about?" Mr. Bagthorpe asked his wife. "What on earth's she talking about?"

Mr. Bagthorpe rarely addressed Mrs. Fosdyke directly if he could help it.

Mrs. Fosdyke was now hedgehogging about the room, weaving in and out between figures already seated on the floor, and placing garlic bulbs at what she considered to be strategic intervals.

"There!" she cried, waving her string of garlic in the manner of a priest swinging incense, "*that*'ll see 'em off!"

"We don't *want* them seeing off, for crying out loud!" Mr. Bagthorpe was beginning to shout again. "We're trying to *raise* 'em, woman!"

Mrs. Fosdyke went tripping heedlessly about the room dispensing her garlic in a style reminiscent of Ophelia strewing flowers.

Mr. Bagthorpe, with an exclamation of fury and disgust, barred her passage and attempted to snatch the string from her grasp. But she held on tightly, and an undignified tug-of-war ensued. In the end the string broke, Mrs. Fosdyke went reeling backward, the garlic scattered and the younger Bagthorpes tittered heartlessly. The law sat silent and bemused. Their police training seemed, at this moment, wholly inadequate.

"Right!" said Mr. Bagthorpe. "Lights out. Doors shut."

"There's still enough to see 'em off, anyhow," muttered Mrs. Fosdyke rebelliously. She sat heavily in her deckchair, still clutching a garlic bulb as talisman. She had already decided to keep her eyes shut throughout.

The light snapped off. Mr. Bagthorpe groped his way back to the circle, cursing as he barked his shin on a stray deckchair.

"Wait for it, old boy!" Jack whispered to Zero.

At first there was only darkness. Then, as their eyes became adjusted, they could make out dim shapes here and there. Grandma, who thought she could already detect a phantom, shut *her* eyes. They all sat silent for what seemed an age. The Bagthorpes, unaccustomed to silence, began to feel uneasy.

"Shouldn't we *say* something?" whispered William to Tess. "Call 'em up, or something? They might not know we're waiting for them."

"Is it all right if I call them, Father?" Tess whispered.

"Do as you like!" came his savage hiss, from the shadows. He felt genuinely jumpy.

"Are the spirits with us tonight?" intoned Tess, in what she considered to be an authentic mediumistic manner.

Silence. Darkness.

"Come, oh Disembodied Skull. . . . Come, oh Bearded Man Carrying a Candle. . . . Come, oh Ring of Blue Fire Wailing. . . . Come, oh . . . come, oh Old Man Limping. . . ."

Hearing this list, Jack could not help feeling that Tess was overdoing things. He personally hoped they would ignore her invitation. He hoped to see only one apparition, at most.

Then, very faintly, he thought he heard voices . . . oddly pitched, talking in snatches. . . . He stiffened and shivered.

My fur's standing on end, he thought.

"Hear that?" came Mr. Bagthorpe's hoarse whisper. He did not sound particularly triumphant. More scared legless.

"Yes!" came back a fervent hiss from all quarters of the room. Mrs. Fosdyke kept her eyes squeezed tight shut, and stuck her fingers in her ears (though without releasing her garlic).

On and on went the distant voices. Sometimes they seemed to break off, at other times there were weird, high-pitched wailing noises.

It must be the Blue Fire, Jack thought. Help!

Moments passed. Nerves tightened. At times the voices seemed to come nearer, only to recede again.

In the end it was Mr. Bagthorpe who cracked. Perhaps he was hypersensitive, as he made out, or perhaps irremediably impatient.

He scrambled to his feet, shouting, "Come on—come on out, whoever you are! Get out here where we can see you!"

He lurched toward the door and threw it open. The seated circle of ghostwatchers saw faintly in the darkness an unmistakable blueness. The voices seemed suddenly louder, crowding the air.

It's coming! thought Jack. The Ring of Blue Fire! Help!

FOURTEEN

The watchers sat breathless, expectant. The blueness seemed to gather strength and glow.

Then came the siren, blasting the silence. All present, with the exception of Mrs. Fosdyke, nearly jumped out of their skins. William clutched at Tess who clutched at Rosie who threw herself onto her mother.

Then, "*Daisy!*" yelled Mr. Bagthorpe in tones of epic fury and despair.

The klaxon blared relentlessly, it was earsplitting. People groped and stumbled to their feet, stiff and cramped. Mr. Bagthorpe was first to reach the front door. Someone found the light switch and they blinked, dazzled.

As they all crowded in the doorway, there came a dull, sickening bang. Daisy had found the hand brake. The police car had rolled back into collision with Uncle Parker's.

In the dazzle the spectators could make out a little, demented figure in the front seat of the squad car, diving this way and that, pushing knobs, pulling switches. Above the crackle of the radio and blare of the siren, they could hear the enraptured squeals of Daisy Parker.

"Wheee! Wheee! Hello hello hello who's zat? This is Daisy Parker talking. Did you hear my bang I jus' made? Have you got any murders? I want a murder!"

On this occasion she was within a whisker of being herself the victim of one. Mr. Bagthorpe was forcibly restrained by

Uncle Parker and Two, while One ran over to the car and switched off the radio and the siren.

"Go 'way! Go 'way!" shrieked Daisy, lashing out at him with her pudgy fists. "You spoiled it now, you spoiled it! I forgot which knobs it was! Where's my people talking gone?"

One pulled Daisy out from the driving seat, tucked her kicking form under his arm and strode back to the others. He plonked her down unceremoniously and she was instantly clasped in Grandma's arms.

"There, my darling child, there!" she cried. Over Daisy's head she fixed the police officers with a quelling glare. "Even the law, it seems," she said in ringing tones, "is not above the persecution of the frail and innocent."

What followed had about it the queer, heightened quality of nightmare, lit as it was by the relentless turning of the blue light.

There was, however, a very strong smell of garlic, which at least lent an air of reality, given that noses rarely figure in nightmares. Mrs. Fosdyke's nails had dug deep into her bulb at the height of her terror. She had definitely suffered more than anyone else, because her encyclopedic knowledge of horror movies had made her aware of what chilling developments were possible. No one else's memory brimmed with so much blood.

The Inquiry that followed Daisy's latest step in the pursuit of knowledge left the earlier one standing. The Bagthorpes, as usual, yelled and screamed. The police officers had lost at a stroke their earlier attitude of detached amusement. As far as they were concerned, Daisy had struck home. The incident with Grandpa had from their point of view been little more than a game, but this, they realized, was another can of worms entirely. Inquiries would be held, official statements would have to be made. Their own demotions were a real and painful possibility. They bitterly regretted ever tangling with the Bagthorpes, in however playful a spirit. (They were not to have known that tangling with the Bagthorpes rarely, if ever, turned out to be playful.)

They inspected the damage to their car. This was not serious, but it was clearly visible. It would have to be entered on a report form, and accounted for.

"How in the name of heaven are we going to explain that it was done by a five-year-old?" asked One despairingly.

"I'll back you up," Mr. Bagthorpe told him. "Are you going to press charges? Any chance of her being locked up?"

The damage to Uncle Parker's car was not serious, either.

"I tell you what," he said to the police officers, "I've just thought up a little scheme. Let you off the hook."

They looked at him hopefully.

"Any disinterested observer," he explained, "seeing the dent at the front of my car and the dent on the back of yours, would naturally assume that I had run into the back of you. Am I right?"

"Perfectly correct, sir," said One.

"So why don't we say that's what happened? Everyone'd believe it. They'd believe it more than if you told the truth."

"They most certainly would," said Mr. Bagthorpe. "Especially if they knew you and the way you drive. The only thing that'd surprise them would be that both vehicles weren't written off."

"I'll say I saw it," volunteered Rosie. "I'll be a witness."

She was worried by her father's suggestion that Daisy might be locked up, and quite ready to perjure herself to prevent this from happening. Uncle Parker's motives for suggesting this deception were far less altruistic. Indeed, he would have been quite happy for Daisy to be remanded in custody for a few days. It would give him a welcome breather. Her behavior of late had been more than usually tiresome.

He had made his apparently generous offer on the principle that one good turn deserves another. If he and his family were to be in this neighborhood for several weeks, then it was all too likely that they would again become involved with the police. This might be as a result of future criminal activities by Daisy, or possibly a motoring offense. Uncle Parker's customary style of driving was the talk of the neighborhood back at home. He drove like a bat out of hell (though one without actual endorsements). His scarlet Austin-Healey was all too eye-catching, and would soon become notorious in Wales, too. It could do him no possible harm, he reasoned, to have some kind of handle with the local police. He did not mean blackmail exactly, but something like it, only legal.

The two policemen were torn. Uncle Parker's offer would let them off the hook entirely. As they stood wrestling with their consciences, a police siren could be heard.

"*Annunner* police!" squealed Daisy, pulling herself free from Grandma's embrace.

Everyone stood listening. The sound became louder, head lamps and a flashing blue light could be seen approaching up the drive. Reinforcements were arriving.

One and Two groaned and went pale. There was no time now to hatch up a convincing story with Uncle Parker. They were hideously discovered.

The second police car drew up and now the air seemed filled with flashing blue light.

All we need is for someone to strike a match, and Daisy's Dragon Water to go up, thought Jack, and we could have the fire brigade as well.

This, given the Bagthorpe tendency not to do things by halves, was definitely in the cards.

And if anyone got burned, he further reflected, an ambulance as well.

It was now midnight and the drive of *Ty Cilion Duon* was a hive of activity. Two more police officers jumped out of the squad car and a whole new round of investigations began.

Numbers Three and Four had been urgently requested by headquarters to go and investigate what had happened to One and Two. This was as a result of Daisy's remarks and messages over the radio. The person on duty who had received these thought it likely that One and Two had been murdered by a maniac who had now taken possession of their squad car and for all anyone knew might start driving all over Wales murdering people. The killer, it was reported, had a high, squeaky voice, which was obviously not his or her real voice, but one put on to confuse the police.

Three and Four, then, were much relieved to find that One and Two were not lying in pools of their own blood. They appeared white and shaken, however, and Jack noticed that the nearside front wing of *their* car was badly crumpled.

"Strewth!" exclaimed Three, mopping his brow. "*That* was a close shave! You two all right? Where's the maniac?"

One and Two were baffled by this query.

"They're *all* maniacs, if you ask me," said One. He, too, had noticed with satisfaction that the second car was far more seriously damaged than his own, whose denting would appear trivial by comparison. "Had an accident?"

"Would you believe us," said Three, "if we told you we'd just seen a ghost?"

"What ghost?" asked Tess jealously.

"We would, as a matter of fact," said One. "Go on. Tell us. We'll buy it. We'll buy anything."

The ghost in question turned out to be Billy Goat Gruff. The two officers had been driving toward *Ty Cilion Duon*, already in a considerable state of jitters. They were, after all, anticipating a meeting with a homicidal maniac. They were both relatively new to the force, and had so far dealt with few things more serious than minor break-ins and motoring offenses. They had nervously been planning what their tactics with this lunatic would be, when Daisy's goat had come out at them from a hedge. The driver had braked and swerved and come into collision with a tree.

As the pair of them sat for a moment, dazed and shaken by the impact, the goat had come dancing into the headlights. They had seen his pink silk ribbons, the bows on his horns, his trailing bells. They had even *heard* his bells, they said.

"If I'd been on my own, I'd never 've believed it," admitted Three.

"Did you run it over?" inquired Mr. Bagthorpe hopefully.

"Certainly not," replied Three. "I took evasive action—hence the damage to the car. We now have to start making inquiries as to its owner."

"Do ghosts have owners?" asked Uncle Parker.

"They are attached, sir, to certain dwellings or lands or properties."

"But can anyone properly be required to keep a *ghost* under proper control?"

"We shall have to look into the exact ramifications of the

law on this point," said Three with dignity. "Someone must be held responsible."

"The animal could, of course, have been the product of your joint imaginations?" suggested Uncle Parker.

"We shall trace its owner," said Four stubbornly.

"Look no further," Mr. Bagthorpe told them treacherously, indicating Uncle Parker with a flourish, and trying to wear a look of careless scorn.

Officers Three and Four looked at Uncle Parker with intense interest. They had briefly speculated as to what kind of person got a goat up to look like that, but had then supposed it to be a person long deceased.

"That the maniac, then?" Three inquired of Two in a hoarse undertone.

"Look," replied Two, "I've already told you. They're *all* maniacs."

"The one with the assumed squeaky voice," Three persisted. "And making death threats over the radio."

"Oh, *that* one!" said Two, enlightened. He indicated Daisy, not without satisfaction. If Daisy had duped headquarters into thinking she was a homicidal maniac, then his own story about the damage to his car would stand up better. It would show that, despite her tender years, she was a force to be reckoned with. Most of the Bagthorpes would have testified to that. They thought of her, more or less, as a Force of Nature.

Mr. Bagthorpe, still going for the careless ease, strolled over and inspected the second squad car.

"Set you back a bit, this will, Russell," he remarked. "Won't have done you much good with the police, either. The police hold grudges for years about this sort of thing."

Uncle Parker did not rise to this.

"Have you noticed," Mr. Bagthorpe continued, "that if a policeman is murdered, they always catch the murderer much quicker than they would if it was just an ordinary citizen?"

Uncle Parker appeared not to hear any of this.

"There is one thing," he murmured. "They may insist that the goat is put down."

Mr. Bagthorpe was unwilling to allow him even this crumb of comfort.

"They won't," he said with conviction. He hated the goat as much as anyone else did, and heartily wished it dead. But he wanted it to go on for as long as possible making Uncle Parker's life a misery.

"An animal has to have two chances," he went on. "If a dog takes a piece out of somebody, you've got to give it another crack of the whip. It has to have taken a piece out of *two* people before it's put down. It may even be three. There's no way round it. It's the law."

Mr. Bagthorpe did not, by and large, care for the law. Indeed, some of his most scathing and best-rehearsed diatribes were reserved for it. Now, it suited him to cite it. He looked over to where the squeaky-voiced homicidal maniac was being interrogated by the police.

"Your daughter is another matter," he said. "I expect she'll be put on remand, awaiting a psychiatrist's report. I, of course, have been advocating one for years. So that's *one* positive thing you can hang on to, Russell. Try to look at it like that. It's an ill wind . . . ."

Daisy's voice broke in at a high, indignant pitch.

"I always press knobs," she was telling the police. "An' my mummy lets me. *An'* she lets me light fires, *an'*. . . ."

Daisy proceeded to catalog a long list of the things Aunt Celia allowed her to do, and ended, "An' I jus' wish my mummy was here!"

"What a mercy that she isn't," Mr. Bagthorpe said to Uncle Parker. "All these blue lights flashing on and off would as sure as God made little apples send *her* right off. As likely as not she would have to be hospitalized."

Rosie was now leaping hither and thither taking flash photographs, and this, combined with the regular flashing of the two blue lights, was beginning to have a disorientating effect on all the Bagthorpes. Mrs. Fosdyke stood on the porch, trying to follow as much as possible of what was going on, in the interests of accurate reportage back at The Fiddler's Arms. She liked to think of herself as more or less the Hansard of The Bagthorpe Saga. The Bagthorpes had had numerous previous entanglements with the police, but so far none of them had been arrested. She was convinced that this luck would now be broken. Also, she did not wish to miss seeing the arrival of the third police car.

One of Mrs. Fosdyke's most firmly held beliefs was that "everything goes in threes." After so many years with the Bagthorpes, she really should have known better. With them, things rarely stopped at three. With them, as soon as two events occurred, they tended to establish a trend.

Given this, the night could well end with half the police squad cars in Wales assembled in the drive of *Ty Cilion Duon* with blue lights flashing.

Grandma was becoming slightly chilled in the night air, but on no account wished to miss anything. She, too, was hoping for an arrest.

"Go and put the kettle on," she told Jack, "and we will all go back inside and talk things over sensibly."

Under no circumstances would she herself have gone back into the house alone. During the séance she felt sure she had sensed an Unseen Presence, and what she was frightened of was that this would materialize into a *Seen* Presence, such as an Old Man Limping, or a Bearded Man Carrying a Candle.

"Gentlemen!" she called. Then again, more loudly, "Gentlemen!"

The four policemen turned.

"Let us all go inside and have some tea," she said.

Policemen One and Two looked dubious at this suggestion. They were reluctant to risk a further séance.

"I think, madam," said One, "that it might be best to postpone inquiries until tomorrow."

"Today, you mean," corrected William.

"I think that would be most unwise," Grandma said. "It is always best to hold inquiries when events are still fresh in witnesses' minds. The evidence is so much more reliable."

This, coming from Grandma, was rich. She could manufacture evidence with the speed and facility of a machine turning out sausages. And all the Bagthorpes, with the exception of Jack, knew well how to arrange events to suit themselves.

Three and Four, whose acquaintance with the Bagthorpes was as yet slight, were more amenable to Grandma's suggestion. They were still shaken from their close shave with Billy Goat Gruff, and felt themselves in need of a hot, sweet drink —if not something stronger.

"Thank you, madam," replied Three. "An excellent suggestion."

And so everyone went inside for the second time that night, and the second Inquiry began.

FIFTEEN

Three and Four, who were not so local as One and Two, and were certainly not related to the Bagthorpes' absentee land-lord, looked about the kitchen in bewilderment.

"Er—nice place you've got here, sir," said Three to Mr. Bagthorpe, assuming him to be the owner.

"It is not nice," he replied curtly, "and it is not mine."

"Rented," explained One quickly. "Ideal holiday home. And haunted."

"Haunted?" repeated Four with evident interest.

"Oh, indubitably," One assured him.

The smell of garlic strengthened. Mrs. Fosdyke, fearing another séance, was digging her nails into her bulb again.

"I think we should confine ourselves to facts," proclaimed Grandma loudly. "I think we should make sworn statements. Is there a Bible in the house?"

At this, something slotted into place in Mrs. Fosdyke's jig-saw of a memory.

" 'Ere!" she said. "It's just come to me. We should've 'ad a Bible before."

They all looked at her.

"They always do," she explained. "What you do, you 'ave a cross round your neck, and garlic in the windows and every-where, and a Bible. You got to take proper precautions."

One and Two, who had been hoping that the subject of the séance would not come up in the presence of their colleagues, coughed uncomfortably.

"You've been Calling Up!" It was Four, in a hoarse, excited tone, eyes glittering. "Calling Up—have you?"

"Not properly," Tess told him. "It was all too makeshift. I am the only one who takes it seriously."

"Ah, indeed, it must be taken seriously," agreed Four, who seemed quite to have forgotten that he was an officer of the law conducting a Preliminary Inquiry. "And you Called Up without a *Bible*?"

He sounded as shocked as if he had been informed that they had intended to make a live sacrifice. He shook his head, long and hard.

"I saw the name on the gate," he said, with an air of deep significance.

There seemed no obvious rejoinder to this, and no one spoke.

"*Ty Cilion Duon.*" He rolled the words off his tongue with relish. He sounded rather like Dylan Thomas reading one of his own poems. "*Ty Cilion Duon.*"

"So what?" demanded Mr. Bagthorpe rudely.

"House of Black Corners!" His voice dropped. "House of Black Corners!"

This, as far as the Bagthorpes were concerned, was a turn up for the book. Nobody had had the time, let alone the inclination, to translate. Now they were momentarily awed. The name certainly had a distinctly sinister ring.

"Black *corners*?" came a disgusted voice. "Black *corners*? There's more than corners black, in this house. Top to bottom, front to back, it'll be all of six weeks before it's put to rights. I've never in all my born days . . . ."

On she rambled. Mrs. Fosdyke's mind was not conspicuously poetic or symbolic. To her, a black corner was, quite literally, a black corner. And she did in fact have a point.

"Are—are *all* the corners black, do you think?" asked Rosie in a small voice. "Even in our bedrooms?"

"There!" exclaimed Tess triumphantly. "It proves my point! The house *is* on a black ley line. It's more than likely on a *meeting* of black lines. The presences in this house will not be pleasant."

At this, Grandma suddenly remembered that she had brought her Bible with her, and sent Jack up to her room to fetch it.

"It is in the far corner by the window," she told him, "and has a photograph of darling Thomas the First on it, and a bunch of dandelions."

Just as Mrs. Fosdyke had her Portable Pantry, so Grandma evidently had her Portable Shrine.

"Come on, Zero," Jack told him, thinking that he would then have a reliable ghost detector in the shape of Zero's fur.

"Put all the lights on while you're up there, won't you?" begged Rosie.

All this talk of Black Corners and apparitions was making most of the Bagthorpes jumpy.

"I am very interested in the supernatural," Four confided. "I have the Sight. Runs in the family, see."

"Look," said Mr. Bagthorpe, "we are not interested in your hobbies, nor those of your next of kin. *Our* interest in the matter is purely scientific. We are engaged in research."

Here there was quite a long silence while Four drew himself up to his not very considerable height.

"Finalist," he said at last in distant tones. "Finalist—Mastermind. Special Subject—The Life and Work of Dennis Wheatley."

"Ooooh!" exclaimed Mrs. Fosdyke admiringly, enchanted

to meet a fellow devotee in so unlikely a context. "There, you see—*'e'll* know about the garlic!"

"Garlic?" said Four. "Certainly. Garlic is of the essence."

"You can say *that* again," remarked Uncle Parker, wrinkling his nose fastidiously.

· "Those that can't stand the garlic," Mr. Bagthorpe told him, "can get out of the kitchen. Ha!"

"Were you really a Finalist in Mastermind?" asked William, impressed. "That means your General Knowledge must be good."

"Father once tried to get on that," Rosie told him. "He chose The Life and Work of Emily Brontë, because she only wrote one novel and some poems. But he didn't score one single point on General Knowledge. Can you believe it? Not *one!*"

"I told you—the questions were rigged," Mr. Bagthorpe snapped. "They always are. They're rigged so that a gravedigger can win, or a dustman or a milk roundsman."

"He didn't even know who invented the telephone," Rosie went on. She started to giggle. "He said Einstein! And when they asked him what a Rhode Island Red was, he said—he said—"

Here she collapsed into helpless giggles. Mr. Bagthorpe had replied that it was a brand of apples, like a Golden Delicious, and had even argued about it when told this answer was wrong. He found this discussion of his General Knowledge— or rather, lack of it—deeply mortifying, and was about to change the subject when Four did so for him.

"When we have the Bible, *I* will Call," he said. "Whom are we Calling?"

"A Small Child Weeping, a Bearded Man Carrying a Candle, a Veiled Lady, a Ring of Blue Fire Emitting—" Tess ticked the list of apparitions off on her fingers.

"I should just Call a couple," William told him. "If all the Corners in this place are Black, there could be dozens of 'em lurking. We don't want the whole shooting match coming out of their corners."

"Ah, Jack dear, thank you!" exclaimed Grandma. She snatched the Bible from his hands, held it aloft, and rattled off, "I swear by Almighty God that the evidence I shall give shall be the truth the whole truth and nothing but the truth so help me God. I wish to testify to Daisy's innocence."

"You realize, don't you, that she's still out there," said Jack.

No one took the slightest notice of him. They all assumed that Daisy had shot her bolt for the night. She had achieved plenty, even by her own exacting standards.

They set about arguing whether they should hold a séance or an Inquiry, or both. One and Two were in favor of holding a very quick Inquiry, and then getting off the premises with the utmost speed possible. Mrs. Fosdyke had changed her position about the séance, and now wanted one, secure in the knowledge that a Dennis Wheatley buff would know how to deploy the garlic properly, and take the necessary precautions to prevent Old Nick himself being inadvertently raised.

It was Four, clearly ecstatic at having come upon what he took to be a whole family of fellow psychics, who carried the day. He had his heart set on an immediate séance and, now that he had his Bible, started organizing it at once.

"Do we have any—Non-Believers?" he asked in sepulchral tones.

Nobody wished to admit to this, largely because they suspected that if they did so they would be ejected from the meeting. They did not feel that they could cope with whatever the Black Corners threw up all alone, and without benefit of Bible and garlic.

"I think Mother should leave the room," said Mr. Bagthorpe. "She is out to sabotage me."

"I think that we should hold the Inquiry first," said Grandma, not troubling to deny this allegation. "I have now sworn my Oath."

"For what it is worth," put in Mr. Bagthorpe.

"I think we ought not to have an Inquiry until I have rigged up the lie detector," Tess said.

"Until you have *what?*" demanded Mr. Bagthorpe.

For her last birthday Tess had asked for, and received, a biofeedback device. She used it, she said, to assist her meditation, but she also claimed that it doubled as a lie detector. This involved electrical wires being taped to the subjects, and so far nobody had accepted Tess's invitation to act as guinea pig.

"I have no wish to be fried alive, thank you," Mr. Bagthorpe had told her, and this more or less summed up the general sentiment. The line between fact and fiction was in any case more than a little blurred for most of the family. They would be poor subjects for a lie detector.

"I could not take part in any Inquiry in which it was even *hinted* that I might tell an untruth," said Grandma piously. "I merely wish to testify to darling Daisy's innocence."

"The Spirits are abroad already! I feel them! I hear them!" Four was now well into his stride and clearly not to be robbed of his séance. "You have Called already, and they have stirred. They have arisen from their Black Corners, and await my bidding!"

"Have they really, d'you think?" Rosie whispered anxiously to Jack.

"I dunno," he whispered back. "But don't worry, there are plenty of us. We'll outnumber them."

"Not if there's one in every corner, we won't. That'll be . . ."—she began to make rapid mental calculations—". . . four bedrooms, four . . . do landings count, d'you think? And the bathroom?"

"We will form a circle," Four was saying, "and I, with the Bible, will take the center."

Things were moving fast.

"It'll be more than *forty!*" whispered Rosie desperately. "Oh, Jack—I'm scared!"

" 'Ere's some garlic, officer," Mrs. Fosdyke said generously, passing him several crushed cloves. The whole room was beginning to smell like a salad dressing.

"Oh, dear, oh, dear—ooooh! I've just remembered something!" Rosie shrieked.

"What, dear?" asked her mother.

"The reports! You haven't opened our reports yet!"

"So we haven't!" exclaimed Mrs. Bagthorpe. "Did you hear that, Henry? We haven't opened the children's reports."

She was evidently herself anxious to postpone the moment when the lights went out again. She had been on the point of suggesting that they have a singsong when Rosie had spoken up. Mrs. Bagthorpe had in the past had several very worrying Problems from people who had dabbled in the supernatural. They had all sounded unhinged, if not downright mad, and she did not wish to see her own family move any further in this direction.

"Hell's *bells*, Laura," expostulated her husband. "You are surely not seriously suggesting—"

"I'll go and get them! They're in my bag! They're in the hall!" Rosie jumped to her feet.

"I don't think there ought to be talk of hell, and such," came Mrs. Fosdyke's doom-laden voice. "Not at a time like this, I don't."

Rosie reached the door and flung it open. As she did so, there came the deafening blast of a police siren—or even two police sirens. The doorway jammed as all present fought to get out.

In the event, only One, Two, Rosie and Mrs. Fosdyke were in time to witness the crash as the second squad car, Daisy energetically turning the wheel, rolled back to meet a third police car rounding the bend in the drive at speed.

There was an almighty bang.

Mr. Bagthorpe shoved unceremoniously to the front and stared wild-eyed at the scene before him. Three blue lights played frenetically over the wreckage. Two police radios crackled and screamed. Two dazed officers staggered from their mangled vehicle.

In the back of the original police car, Grandpa was still sitting with the beatific smile of a man who has just seen his dearest wish come true.

"I said so," came Mrs. Fosdyke's lugubrious tones. "Didn't I say so? Things always go in threes."

Mr. Bagthorpe began to sneeze.

The second day of the Bagthorpes' holiday was taken up with police interviews, mainly. Many and lengthy statements had to be made, and even at the end of the day no very clear picture of the events of the previous night emerged. This was because most of the statements (though all, naturally, were signed and sworn as being true) were conflicting.

Mr. Bagthorpe blamed Daisy Parker and, by implication, Uncle Parker and the police themselves.

"There was no need," he asserted, "for them to descend at dead of night on a quiet, holiday-making family as if they had been tipped off that someone was running drugs or plotting the assassination of the Prime Minister."

Uncle Parker, Grandma, Rosie and Daisy herself held Daisy to be totally innocent. This was an almost impossible position to take, given that Daisy had single-handedly dented one police car and written off two others, but they took it anyway.

Everybody else blamed Daisy Parker and her goat, though Mrs. Bagthorpe was held to be a not very reliable witness because she had been suffering from shock at the time, having just had about two gallons of rainwater squeezed over her.

Matters were further complicated by the arrival at *Ty Cilion Duon* of Aunt Celia, dressed as if she were going to a fancy dress party as the Lady of Shalott. She certainly acted as if a curse had come upon her, though she did not, fortunately, faint. She was highly strung at the best of times (not to say unstable, as Mr. Bagthorpe *did* say) and a generous dose of cold water administered by Mrs. Fosdyke would probably have finished her off.

Aunt Celia was certainly very soulful, but she must also have had a modicum of native cunning, because she went all out to enlist the sympathy and support of the police. This was not difficult, because she was ravishingly beautiful and could also, seemingly at will, weep large, glistening tears that rolled appealingly down her cheeks without making either her eyes or nose red.

"Spare a thought for a mother's grief," she entreated. "Do not blight a mother's life."

Grandma used more straightforward tactics—namely, blackmail.

"I should imagine that the chief constable of this county

would be much interested to hear that two out of three of the crashes took place while the officers concerned were playing parlor games," she told them. "I should not be surprised," she went on, "if the Home Secretary would not be interested to learn this. It is, I take it, no part of an officer's brief to raise spirits from the dead while on duty?"

Here she had four of the six policemen floored. Grandma had a very nice line in cross-examination. She got this partly from all the police serials she watched on television and partly from years of practice in the Inquests and Post Mortems regularly held by the Bagthorpes themselves.

The police would have gladly washed their hands of the whole affair, had this been feasible, and dropped their inquiries. Unfortunately, the mangled state of their vehicles made this impossible. Grandma's own sworn statement would, if believed by their superiors, get them all severely reprimanded if not actually drummed out of the force. In it she alleged that Officers One and Two had invited Daisy to play with their car and shown her how the radio worked, and that Three and Four had refused to leave the house until they had raised a spirit. She also said that the third police car had come up the drive at ninety miles an hour. She rounded off her statement by alleging that the police had intimidated a minor —namely Daisy.

Mrs. Fosdyke's statement was extremely diffuse. She saw her chance to report all Daisy's previous misdemeanors, going back years. When the police weakly pointed out that Daisy's setting fire to Grandma's Birthday Party had no bearing on the present case, she argued with them.

"Criminals always have a long list of things they've done previous," she told them. "They ask the judge to take 'em into account. I do read the papers, you know."

The real reason, of course, was that Mrs. Fosdyke found it very therapeutic to list all Daisy's crimes on a police form. She had longed to do this for years, and was now determined that Daisy's police record should be as comprehensive as possible. She also gave at great length her own opinion of Daisy and her character.

"It's facts we want," Three told her. "Not opinions."

This cut no ice with Mrs. Fosdyke, who saw no distinction between the two.

By the time the statements were completed, all involved were feeling extremely jaded. The Bagthorpes gathered in the porch to watch the last breakdown truck winching up a police vehicle. The dispirited police made their departure.

"Come an' play annunner time!" Daisy squealed after them.

And there the scene freezes. There is never really an ideal moment to pause for a while in the telling of The Bagthorpe Saga. Natural breaks are few and far between, climaxes commonplace. We leave the Bagthorpes and their victims locked in tableau, eerily moveless and silent, and behind them, the looming shadow of the House of Black Corners.

The secrets of those Corners, and much else besides (including the tracking down of Daisy's goat) must await the unfolding of yet another grisly chapter of The Bagthorpe Saga. . . .